"I gave it a try and I liked it," Mina said with a note of humor in her voice. **"I've always been a physical person and this life suits me."**

Jake inhaled and exhaled. The clean mountain air was invigorating. "I can see what you mean. This is the life."

Mina laughed softly. "I'm glad you like it. You know you could be in a luxurious suite at Harrah's Cherokee Casino Resort. They have over 1,100 rooms, plus a casino and a world-class entertainment center where top country music artists perform every weekend—"

Jake leaned over and kissed her midsentence. He let her lead him, waiting for permission to deepen the kiss. He would have been satisfied with just the taste of her lips on his tongue. After a moment, Mina sighed softly and gave herself to him. Her hand came up to caress his cheek, and she leaned in to him. Jake marveled at how sweet she tasted and how well the two of them anticipated each other's needs. It was a gentle kiss. It was a kiss to seal what they each knew was happening between them, a meeting of kindred souls.

Books by Janice Sims

Harlequin Kimani Romance

Temptation's Song
Temptation's Kiss
Dance of Temptation
A Little Holiday Temptation
Escape with Me
This Winter Night
Safe in My Arms

JANICE SIMS

is the author of twenty-one novels and has had stories included in nine anthologies. She has been nominated for a Career Achievement Award by *RT Book Reviews,* and her novel *Temptation's Song* was nominated for Best Kimani Romance Series in 2010 by *RT Book Reviews.* A longtime member of Romance Writers of America, she lives in Central Florida with her family.

JANICE SIMS

SAFE IN *My* ARMS

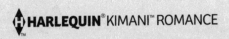
HARLEQUIN® KIMANI™ ROMANCE

This book is dedicated to my Yahoo group who has shown a great deal of loyalty over the years. You're like an extended family. Thanks for being the kind of readers who not only write reviews all over the web, but have been known to make new converts by word-of-mouth.

Recycling programs
for this product may
not exist in your area.

ISBN-13: 978-0-373-86355-6

SAFE IN MY ARMS

Copyright © 2014 by Janice Sims

For questions and comments about the quality of this book please contact us at CustomerService@Harlequin.com.

Printed in U.S.A.

www.Harlequin.com

Dear Reader,

What makes a hero? Are they born with a sense of duty to others? Or do heroes simply react when the time comes to step up and save someone? In *Safe in My Arms,* both Amina Gaines and Jake Wolfe have suffered severe personal losses and are scarred by them.

We all have scars. None of us go through life without being marked by them. It's up to us whether or not those scars add to our character or detract from it. That's what I found so fascinating about Mina and Jake: they were people who rose above misfortune and thrived. An accident brought them together, but what happened after that was no accident—it was Fate.

I'm presently writing the third book in the Gaines Sisters series. You can contact me via Facebook, www.janicesims.com, Jani569432@aol.com or at Post Office Box 811, Mascotte, Florida 34753-0811.

Janice

Acknowledgments

Thanks to both Shannon Criss and Rachel Burkot
for their editorial expertise in the production of
Safe in My Arms. Your insights were most appreciated.

Chapter 1

"Oh, my God," cried John Monahan, his face set in grim lines and his eyes on the Piper Matrix G1000's fuel gauge. The indicator was perilously close to empty. "Somebody's tampered with the fuel line. We don't have enough to make it to the next town, let alone Atlanta."

Jake Wolfe, sitting next to him in the pilot's seat, stared at him in disbelief. John had gone pale under his tan. Jake felt his stomach plummet as he leaned over to peer out of the side window. Although John had the plane in a controlled glide, it felt as if the forest of the Great Smoky Mountains was rising up to meet them.

"We still have time to jump!" he said while unfastening his seat belt. When he had been loading the plane earlier today he'd spotted a couple of parachutes in the overhead storage compartment.

"It's worth a try," said John, sounding far from confident.

Hope blossomed in Jake's chest when he found the parachutes. But on closer inspection, he discovered the rip cords on both of them had been irreparably damaged.

He hurried back to his seat and buckled up. "They're totally useless," he reported to John.

"It's my fault," John said gloomily as he did everything in his power to slow their descent. "I called Lynn and told her what I was planning to do. I never suspected Charlie would bug my home phone. I put Lynn at risk."

"Don't worry about that right now," Jake said tightly. He was trying not to panic. It wasn't working. "Just concentrate on landing this thing."

A DEA agent, Jake had been undercover for nearly a year to get evidence on Charlie Betts, one of the most notorious drug dealers in the southern United States. The agency had never been able to catch him with the goods. But now, here Jake was, in a plane with its cargo hold stuffed full of illegal drugs recently obtained in Canada and a pilot willing to testify against Betts, and they were going down!

John was still talking nervously as he worked furiously to land the plane in a clearing he'd spotted below.

"I can't believe Charlie would sabotage a million-dollar plane and risk millions of dollars' worth of product going up in smoke just to get rid of me."

Jake figured John was talking to calm himself, so he joined in the conversation, even though he felt that discussing anything right now, other than how to save their lives, was counterproductive. "You sound hurt, John. What did you expect from a murdering bastard like Charlie Betts?"

John turned to look at him for a split second, fear and anguish in his eyes. "The clearing's a no-go, but I'm going to get this baby down in one piece, one way or another, and if I don't make it, take care of my family. I shouldn't have told Lynn. I'm such a fool."

"The agency's been watching over your family for weeks now, ever since I suspected you were coming over to our side," Jake told him. "And we're *both* gonna make it." He nodded at the controls. "Ground's coming up fast. Work your magic, John."

"Hold on!" John yelled. The plane careened into a pine forest. The sound of the crash was deafening. Shards of glass flew around them like sparkling rain. The nose of the plane slid down a huge tree trunk to the forest floor, and then the plane fell onto its back, which was lucky for them, because the fuel tank was on the bottom of the plane. That, and the fact that the tank was nearly empty when they crashed, saved them from an explosion. Jake didn't have time to brace himself. His final thought before losing consciousness was that if he was going to die he hoped it would happen quickly.

* * *

"I know what you're up to, Grandpa," Amina Gaines said accusingly as she trailed her grandfather up a steep slope. He had an amazing energy level for someone in his eighties. "Getting me out here on the pretense of scouting new camping sites for the guests is just a ruse to keep me from watching CNN, totally spoiling my Thursday morning routine."

"All that talk about the troops pulling out of Afghanistan just brings back bad memories for you," Grandpa Beck said matter-of-factly. He paused, looked back at her and breathed in the clear, fresh mountain air. "This," he said, his arms spread wide to include all of nature, "is so much better for you. Besides, the place I'm going to show you will be a good hiking destination when we open up again next week."

Mina laughed shortly. She had to admit that living and working with her grandfather at his lodge had been good for her. She had spent ten years of her life in the military. Four years at a military academy and six years as an army helicopter pilot. Her last hitch had been in Afghanistan where she'd lost the love of her life, Keith Armstrong, who was killed by an improvised explosive device. After Keith's death, her heart was no longer in making the military her chosen career. So, when her hitch was over, she had not re-upped. Now she felt kind of like a fish out of water. But the past year or so, up here near the Cherokee reservation and the Great Smoky Mountains, her soul had felt more at home than it had in a very long time.

She smiled at her grandfather. He was a trim man of average height with long, wavy snow-white hair that he wore pulled back in a ponytail. His weather-beaten brown skin was the color of well-worn leather. In his youth he'd been a handsome man. He was still striking, although, as he liked to say, he'd earned every wrinkle on his face and he was proud of them.

"Stop grinning, and keep moving," Grandpa Beck ordered brusquely, turning to continue their trek. "We've got a couple more miles to go before we reach that ridge I was telling you about."

Mina paused to grab a bottle of water from her backpack. Drinking deeply, she peered up at the crystalline-blue September sky and spotted a plane coming toward them. Its trajectory was way off. It was flying far too low to even clear some of the tops of the nearby trees.

As it got closer she could hear its engines. Her pilot's ears told her the plane was definitely in distress. That intermittent sputter or hitch in the engine was not normal.

Her grandfather was watching it, too, a frown marring his features. "Is it supposed to sound like that?" he asked.

Mina was paying close attention to the plane while putting her water bottle away and securing her backpack. "No, it's not. I think they're going down."

"Are you sure?" Benjamin hesitated. "Maybe it can still get control of itself."

Then the sound of the engine went completely silent, the plane disappeared from view, and they heard the thunderous boom of a crash. A look passed between granddaughter and grandfather. They knew that they quite possibly could mean the difference between life and death for the occupants of that plane.

Mina took out her cell phone to see if she could get a signal. Just as she had suspected, there was none. There were no cell phone towers in the vicinity.

"Grandpa," said Mina as she stuck the phone in her jacket pocket. "We can't call anybody, so you need to get back to the lodge and contact the forest rangers or mountain rescue. I'm going to the crash site to see if there are any survivors."

"The site could be miles away," Benjamin protested. "And we're at least five miles from the lodge. I should stay with you in case we have to carry someone out of here."

Mina was shaking her head. "There could be more than one survivor. Plus, I'm going to have to hustle, and I can make better time without you," she told him frankly. "You know these mountains. If anyone can point the rescuers in the right direction, it's you."

Benjamin reluctantly nodded in agreement. He went into his backpack and handed over his extra water and energy bars. "You might need these before it's over with."

Mina accepted his provisions and shoved them into her backpack. "I'm going now," she said. "Be careful going back down the mountain, Grandpa."

"I'll be okay," Benjamin said. "You're the one walking into an unknown situation. Better put on your captain persona, baby girl."

Mina smiled at him and gave him a thumbs-up before turning and rapidly walking in the direction in which she'd seen the plane go down.

Captain was the rank she'd earned while in the army. No one had called her that in two years.

After half an hour, she realized that even though she could guess in which direction the plane's wreckage could be found, she needed more accurate information than that to go on. So she decided to climb a tree to see if she could spot the downed plane from above. It had been a while since she'd had to scale a tree, although she and her sisters had done it all the time when they were kids, and she had done it on weekends as part of endurance training while in the army.

Removing her backpack and dropping it onto the ground beneath a fifty-foot pine tree, she put on the supple leather fingerless gloves that she had in her backpack to protect her hands while rock climbing. She kept her jacket on to protect her arms and chest from the rough bark of the tree. She removed her rubber-soled hiking boots and thick socks because bare feet gave her more traction. She took hold of the tree trunk and shinnied up the tree enough to grasp an upper branch. Then she carefully climbed from branch to branch until she was about thirty feet up. Muscles she had forgotten she had burned with the effort. She looked around. There, to the south, was the plane resting on its back. She didn't see any rising plumes of smoke, which she figured was a good thing.

Getting down out of the tree was much easier than

climbing it. She put her socks and boots back on, secured her backpack and began jogging in the direction of the crash site.

She glanced down at her watch as she ran. It was a few minutes after one in the afternoon, several hours before sundown. She and Grandpa Beck had gotten an early start this morning. Hopefully their early start would bode well for any survivors of the crash. Search and rescue would have a more difficult time finding them in the dark. Plus, this being autumn in the mountains, nights could get very cold.

Leaning into her sprint, she ran on, praying all the while that when she reached the site she would find someone alive.

Jake groaned as he came to. For a moment, his vision was blurry. When his eyes did finally focus, everything still appeared screwy to him. Then he realized he was upside down. He was afraid to move in case something was broken. So he stayed still and took a mental inventory of his body. Where did it hurt? *Pretty much everywhere* was his answer. "John?"

His voice was barely a whisper. "John!" No reply.

"John, if you can hear me, please say something!"

No sounds issued from John Monahan. Jake sighed in despair.

His vision clearer now, he looked around. Shattered glass, pine needles, broken branches and wrapped bundles of drugs littered the floor. No, not the floor, he remembered. It was the ceiling of the plane, because they were upside down.

He took a couple of deep breaths. He couldn't stay here like this. What if no one had seen them go down? Some parts of these mountains were very isolated. There was a possibility that the only way he was getting out of this predicament was by his own efforts.

First he had to figure out which, if any, parts of him were injured. So he started by wiggling his fingers and toes. All moved normally. Then he tried moving his arms and legs. Once again, they seemed in good shape. Next he turned his head. That was when he saw poor John slumped to the side with a tree branch stuck in his chest. Jake viciously cursed the fates. It wasn't fair. The guy was trying to turn his life around. Now he was dead for doing the right thing.

Jake vowed that Charlie Betts would pay for this.

With new resolve, he reached over to unfasten his seat belt, realizing that as soon as he did so, he would fall to the roof of the plane. He anticipated a lot of pain when he did so, but he had no alternative.

Just as he was about to click the release button, he heard a noise. It sounded like someone was trying to force the door open. Then he could have sworn he heard a muffled voice on the other side of the door.

Mina pulled hard on the door. It seemed to be jammed. She braced one foot on the side of the plane and put her back into it. The door popped open suddenly, throwing her off balance and onto her backside.

She got up and pulled the door all the way open and peered inside. "Hello, can anyone hear me?"

"Yeah, thank God, I can hear you!"

Mina gingerly stepped inside. The ceiling of the plane was covered in padded leather the same neutral tone as the interior's six seats. She stepped around bundles of something that appeared to have been put in opaque garbage bags and then wrapped with duct tape for added security. Glass and pine needles and various-sized tree branches crunched underfoot.

"Are you alone?" she asked the man who had answered her.

"No, the pilot's here beside me," he said. "Please check him. He hasn't said anything since I regained consciousness."

"Okay, I'm getting closer," Mina told him. Momentarily she was right beside him. As he'd asked, she checked the pilot first. She was horrified by the sight of the tree branch sticking out of his chest, but that didn't stop her from feeling for a pulse. She'd seen worse-looking injuries in Afghanistan, and some of those soldiers had actually survived them. So she was thorough about checking for signs of life.

"I'm sorry," she said after a couple of minutes, her tone solemn. "Your friend is gone."

She heard a sharp intake of breath from the survivor and then a long exhale. "I was hoping I was wrong and he'd made it," he said.

Mina moved close beside him as he hung upside down in his seat, and that was when he got a good look at her. She was twentysomething, about five-

five, and slender. To him she had the face of an angel, a black angel with golden-brown skin and abundant black hair that she wore in braids down her back.

"Are you the advance person of a team of rescuers?" he joked.

Mina smiled as she began running her hand across his body, trying to ascertain the nature of his injuries. "My grandfather and I were hiking in the mountains when we saw your plane go down. We couldn't get a cell-phone signal, so he's on the way back down the mountain to notify the authorities. Until they get here, I'm all you've got."

"It's not that I don't appreciate your help," Jake said, "but I weigh two hundred pounds. I don't think you could carry me if I'm unable to walk."

Mina was still running her hands over his body. "Does anything on you hurt when I touch you?"

For a moment Jake forgot about the pain. He thought that must be a good sign. That a pretty woman could make him forget he'd just been in a plane crash. "I don't think I have any broken bones," he told her. "If you can help me out of this seat, I believe I can walk out of here under my own steam."

"All right," she agreed immediately. "I'm going to get close to you and spot you. You unfasten the seat belt on a count of three."

Their eyes met. Mina's dark brown eyes were encouraging. His probably looked doubtful. "Whenever you're ready," Mina said confidently.

Jake took a deep breath, counted out loud to three

and hit the release button. Gravity did the rest. But what he had anticipated would be a painful experience was not, because the woman whom he had thought was not strong enough to carry him was supporting him securely in her arms. His legs felt weak initially, and when he felt the blood trickling down the bridge of his nose, he realized that he had a head injury. Being upside down, he had not noticed the blood. His hand went to his head.

The woman smiled at him. "It doesn't look bad," she told him. "I'll take a look at it when we get outside."

Jake's legs felt stronger. Believing he could walk now, he gestured toward the door with a nod of his head. "Maybe we should get out of here. We've been lucky so far because the plane was nearly out of fuel when we crashed, but who knows?"

"I'm ready when you are," Mina said.

They walked slowly to the exit, and Mina helped him step out of the plane onto the forest floor. He squinted up at the sky. It had taken Mina nearly three hours to reach the crash site after she'd spied it from her perch in the pine tree.

"Somehow I thought the sun would be lower in the sky," he said. "It feels as though I've been in there for hours."

"Only three hours," Mina assured him as they continued walking away from the plane. "It was a bit after one when I heard the crash, and I got here about three hours later."

He looked down at her in amazement. "I can't believe you did that. You had no idea what you could be walking into. What made you do it?"

"Let's find you a safe place to sit down before I tell you my life story, okay?" Mina said lightly.

Chapter 2

"Easy," Mina cautioned as she helped the stranger sit down with his back against a sugar maple tree. They were out of the copse of pines in which the plane had crashed. Mina thought it wise to put some distance between them and the plane. He'd mentioned that the fuel had been depleted before the crash, but better safe than sorry.

She saw that the scratch on his forehead was still bleeding and shrugged off her backpack to look inside for something with which to stanch the bleeding. "I wonder if there's a first-aid kit on the plane," she mused as she searched. She didn't relish having to go back on board where this man's friend was still hanging upside down with a tree branch stuck in his chest, but she would do it if she couldn't get the blood to stop flowing.

She found a clean paper towel and pressed it firmly against the two-inch-long cut. The stranger was looking at her with a hint of humor in his gaze.

"We haven't introduced ourselves," he said softly. "Hello, I'm Jake, and you are?"

"You can call me Mina," she said.

"Whenever someone introduces themselves like that, there's usually another name that they're trying to conceal," he observed with a smile.

"It's short for Amina," she said.

"One letter short," he joked. "Wow."

Mina laughed. She liked his accent. He wasn't Southern, that was for sure. He sounded like a New Yorker. "I suppose Jake's short for Jacob?"

"No, Jason. I know it should be short for Jacob, but Jake's what my parents started calling me and it stuck."

"Like mine, only one letter shorter," Mina noted.

"You're sharp," he said.

"You've been hit on the head," she countered. "It doesn't take much to be sharper than you are right now."

"And beautiful," he added.

"The head thing again," she said.

He ignored her. "Where are we, Mina?"

"You're near a little town called Cherokee, close to the Tennessee/North Carolina border. Where were you headed?"

"Atlanta."

"You're quite a few miles away," Mina told him as she continued to press the paper towel to his forehead.

"What are you, a businessman? That Piper Matrix is some sweet plane."

"You know planes?"

"I was a helicopter pilot when I was in the army."

"How long since you were discharged?"

"Going on two years," she answered.

"What was your rank when you left?"

"I was a captain," she stated simply.

"I'm impressed," he said. "I was in the army for a couple of years but did it mainly for the educational benefits." He looked into her eyes. "Sit, Mina. Please."

But she wouldn't sit. "Are you thirsty?" she asked. "There's water in my backpack."

"I could use a drink," he said. But before she could retrieve the water he reached up and grasped her hand. While he had hold of it, he brought it down to eye level and said, "Your hands are so small, but extremely competent. Is that you in a nutshell, Mina, small but extremely competent?"

Mina found both his words and his touch disconcerting. She pried her hand from his and got the water bottle her grandfather had given her earlier.

He opened it and drank deeply, still looking into her eyes. "Thank you."

"You're welcome," said Mina. She removed the paper towel from his forehead. The cut had stopped bleeding.

"I guess I won't have to go back into the plane, after all," she said. "You're not bleeding anymore."

He smiled at her. "I'm a fast healer."

* * *

In truth, he didn't want her to go back inside the plane. If she hadn't already noticed the bundles strewn all over it and begun to put two and two to-gether—a private plane with mysterious, securely wrapped packages as the main cargo—he would con-sider himself lucky. His rescuer seemed to be a very intelligent woman. And he didn't want her getting mixed up in this mess. At this point, he didn't know what his next move was going to be. He had to con-tact the agency. She'd said her cell phone didn't work up here. There was no reason to believe his would either. He didn't have a satellite phone. No harm in trying his cell, though.

He still felt it in the back pocket of his jeans. He was surprised it hadn't fallen out of his pocket while he was upside down. Tight jeans, he guessed.

Try as he might, Jake couldn't get a signal. He sighed inwardly. What would he say to his boss, any-way? John Monahan was dead. And there was no bringing him back. He had failed to protect a witness. John might have worked in Betts's organization for years, but he was trying to clean up his act for the benefit of his wife and two small children. It irked Jake that he hadn't been able to anticipate someone tampering with the plane. But John had been a con-scientious pilot. Jake had seen him examining the plane before climbing into the cockpit.

If John had missed signs of tampering, how could he have recognized them? Still, he blamed himself for

John's death. And he meant to make sure that justice was served in the end.

He scowled as he tucked the useless phone back in his pocket. Mina noticed and frowned in response. "No luck, huh?"

"Nah, but it can wait." His stomach growled. He smiled wryly. "You wouldn't have something to eat in that handy backpack, would you?"

Mina smiled warmly and dug in her backpack a moment.

They were companionably eating energy bars beneath the sugar maple when they heard the rotors of a helicopter in the distance.

Benjamin Beck hated two modes of transportation: riding on a bus and flying. The UH-60 Black Hawk he was in now was being piloted by a young hotshot from the Army National Guard. Two other Guardsmen made up the team. Ben was sitting up front with the pilot giving directions. The Great Smoky Mountains looked a lot different from the air, but Ben had never gotten lost in his life. Soon, they were hovering over the area where he'd last seen Mina more than five hours ago. He looked at the pilot and said, "Try due south. That was the direction the plane was heading when she was going down."

Less than five minutes later they spotted it.

"Looks like a Piper Matrix," said the pilot with admiration. "Nice plane."

Ben was busy craning his neck, trying to locate Mina. He hoped nothing had happened to that girl.

He had not wanted to leave her, but her plan of action had clearly been the only option for them at the time.

His heartbeat accelerated with excitement and happiness when he saw her sitting propped against a tree, a big guy sitting beside her. "There they are!" Ben exclaimed, pointing and grinning.

The pilot grinned too. "So I see," he said. "I'm going to set her down in that clearing over there."

It was dark by the time the Black Hawk rose into the air again. One of the Guardsmen was a medic and had examined Jake and determined his vital signs were good, and except for his head injury, he was fine. Then the Guardsmen removed John Monahan's body from the wreckage, put it in a body bag and stowed it in the back of the Black Hawk.

Mina and Grandpa Beck stood apart talking while all of this was going on, but she didn't fail to notice Jake speaking privately with the helicopter's pilot and the keen look of interest on the pilot's face during the course of their conversation. She also noticed that one of the Guardsmen came out of the plane carrying one of those wrapped bundles Mina had avoided stepping on when she'd entered the downed plane and presented it to the helicopter pilot, who told him to leave it on the plane.

That made her wonder what was in those bundles that made them not important enough to salvage from the wreckage. There had been about thirty twenty-four-inch cubes. Or maybe, she thought, there was something in them that Jake didn't want the National

Guardsmen to know about, and during his conversation with the pilot he'd convinced him that they weren't worth bothering with.

Her curiosity was definitely engaged. She was a sucker for a good mystery, and this had the potential for becoming a brain twister.

When the pilot announced it was time to board the Black Hawk, she hesitated. "I think I'll walk out of here," she told him.

"Mina, you're exhausted," Jake was quick to say. "I'm not going anywhere until you get in this helicopter."

"He's right," her grandfather seconded. "It's been a long day. Let's go home, child."

Knowing she'd been outvoted, Mina relented. But she would have dearly loved to have been left alone with those bundles to see what was in them. Her grandfather's concern for her well-being, she knew, was genuine. But she suspected Jake was more concerned about leaving her alone with those mysterious packages aboard the downed Matrix.

She sat next to Jake on the flight to Cherokee. He tried to make polite conversation, but she barely heard him because her mind was so consumed with the distinct possibility that the man she'd rescued was a drug dealer. Why hadn't she seen it before now? A private plane filled with packages wrapped in garbage bags? Two men on board, one a pilot, one a… what? she wondered. What was Jake's role in all of this? Was he the hired gun?

She observed him as they flew through the now

darkened sky toward Cherokee. He was so hand-some. He looked to be in his mid-thirties, and when he smiled, dimples appeared in both caramel-brown cheeks. He had perfect teeth, a square-chinned, clean-shaven face that now had a five-o'clock shadow, nice ears, an interesting nose with a small scar on the bridge and curly dark-brown hair that was cut close to his perfect head. And when he looked at her, there was nothing but warmth and sincerity in those warm honey-colored eyes. He could be the all-American boy next door. Big, athletic, superbly muscled and with a personality to match. But he could also be a cold-blooded killer who ran drugs for a living.

He smiled at her now. "I don't know how I can repay you for what you did for me today," he said, eyes shining with good intentions.

"I'm just sad that there was nothing we could do for your friend," Mina said. Too many times, while in the service of her country, she'd had to transport the bodies of fallen soldiers. This situation gave her a cold feeling inside. Her sister, Desiree, who was a psychotherapist, wanted her to go to therapy, say-ing that even if she didn't believe she was suffering from post-traumatic stress disorder, there could still be residual aftereffects from her experiences in the military. She shouldn't be too proud to seek help. But Mina knew she was fine. It was only a few times a year, like today, that she was reminded of the nega-tive aspects of military life.

"Me, too," Jake said softly. "I dread having to tell his wife. They have two small kids."

"Did you know him well?"

"We'd only been working together for a few months, but he was a nice guy, devoted to his family."

Devoted to his family, Mina thought. Would a guy who loved and cherished his family be working as a pilot for a drug dealer? She wasn't naive. Of course a man could love his family and be a criminal.

They didn't have time to finish their conversation, because in a matter of minutes the Black Hawk, which could reach a hundred and sixty miles per hour, was landing in a big field adjacent to her grandfather's lodge. The pilot explained they'd be going on to Asheville where Jake would be checked out by a doctor at Mission Hospital.

Before Mina and her grandfather could go, though, Jake grasped Mina by the hand. "I don't want to lose touch with you, Mina. Give me your number, please. I'd like to call you when I come back this way."

Mina met his eyes. Did she want this man who could be a drug dealer to phone her? Was she being too judgmental? She had no proof he was a dealer, just a suspicion that could probably be blamed on reading too many suspense novels.

He handed her his cell phone. "Would you enter your number for me?"

She took it, quickly tapped out her number and handed it back to him. "Stay safe, Jake."

He gave her that killer smile and then turned and went back to the waiting helicopter.

She and Grandpa Beck watched as they rose into the sky and sped off. Her grandfather put his arm around her shoulders as they walked to the cabin in back of the lodge where they lived. The lodge was set to reopen next week for the fall season. Guests would start arriving on Sunday afternoon. Soon they would be busy catering to the needs of hunters, fishermen, hikers and a host of other nature lovers.

"I don't know about you," Grandpa Beck said, "but I'm hungrier than a bear at the end of hibernation."

Mina laughed and said, "Come on, then, I'll make you some scrambled eggs and bacon."

"Breakfast for dinner," Grandpa Beck said, grinning. "Now you're talking!"

As the helicopter rose in the air, Jake watched the figures of Mina Gaines and her grandfather recede into the distance. He didn't know why, but being near her gave him a warm feeling deep inside. It was a cliché, but he felt as though they had been fated to meet.

He turned and looked straight ahead as the pilot cranked up the speed of the Black Hawk and shot toward Asheville. This case had taken a turn for the worse when he'd been so close to wrapping it up.

He worked out of the Atlanta Division of the Drug Enforcement Administration, which served the states of Georgia, Tennessee, North Carolina and South Carolina. He'd infiltrated the Charlie Betts drug ring by first ingratiating himself with the big guy. He'd had Betts under surveillance for weeks and had followed him to his favorite nightclub one evening, when a drunken reveler had had the audacity to attempt to slug the drug dealer. Before Betts's own bodyguard had the chance to act, Jake had stepped between the drunk and Betts. Impressed with his physical prowess, Betts had given Jake his card and told him if he ever needed anything to call him. The next day, Jake called and said he was down on his luck and could use a job. Betts hired him as low-level muscle.

He'd worked his way up to accompanying John on the weekly flights to Canada, where Betts's marijuana supplier lived. He and Monahan had become friends, and Monahan had confided in him that he wanted out of the organization—but there was only one way out: death. That was when Jake had offered him another alternative: testify against Charlie Betts, and Jake would stand up for him and try to get him immunity.

That's what they were attempting to do when the Matrix had gone down. They had a plane full of marijuana as evidence against Charlie Betts.

Jake was angry at himself for not anticipating that Charlie Betts had tapped John's home phone. He should have cautioned John against telling anyone about their plans, even his wife, Lynn. Jake blamed himself for John's death. He would do everything in his power to make John's sacrifice mean something. That meant Betts and his organization had to go down.

Once they'd landed in Asheville and he'd seen John's body being taken to the morgue, Jake got on the phone with the Special Agent in Charge in Atlanta.

Hoyt Granger was in his fifties and had a gravelly voice due to too many cigarettes, a habit he was constantly trying to kick. "Jake, what the hell happened to you? You were supposed to report in hours ago!"

Jake told him everything, and then patiently waited for his response.

"Thank God you're safe," Granger said. "My guess is Betts expected you and Monahan to go up in flames. That didn't happen, so now we have ourselves a predicament. When word reaches Betts, and I'll make sure it does, will he send his men to retrieve the drugs or write millions of dollars off just like that? I'm betting he'll want to recover what he believes to be rightfully his. So you need to stick around. Stay out of sight. It might be to your advantage if Betts thinks you didn't survive so I'm going to spread the news that both you and Monahan died in the crash."

"You're leaving the drugs at the site as bait?" Jake asked, to be certain they were on the same page.

"That's right," Granger confirmed. "Get back to Cherokee, hole up in a motel and I'll send you the needed equipment, a sat phone and some heavy artillery. I'll have agents and a helicopter waiting for your call after you catch Betts's men in the act. As soon as we have them in custody, Betts will be arrested, too."

"Sounds like you've got it all planned out," said Jake with a note of skepticism.

"Can't go as belly-up and ass-backward as the last plan did," Granger commented dryly.

"Cherokee's a small town," Jake said. "I've met some of the people." He was thinking about Mina and her grandfather. "They're nice people. I don't want them to get caught in the middle of a drug fight."

"Then make sure there aren't any confrontations in town, Jake. Follow Betts's guys into the woods. Take them down there."

"Got it," Jake said. He knew there was no use arguing with Granger when he had his mind made up. "I'll let you know where to send the needed equipment."

They said their goodbyes, and Jake put his cell phone away with a grimace. Granger sat in his office all day, issuing orders. He hadn't been in the field in so long, he'd forgotten that real people were out here. People they'd taken an oath to protect.

Two hours later, after being released from the hospital with a prescription for pain pills and the suggestion to take it easy for a couple days, Jake checked into a hotel in Asheville, took a hot shower and then crashed for the night.

Tomorrow he would rent a car and head back to Cherokee.

Chapter 3

On Sunday morning, Mina was on a ladder polishing the twin wooden totem poles that flanked the entrance to the lodge. She made it a habit of doing this last task just before new arrivals were expected. The two-story entrance never failed to impress the guests who thought the intricately carved door, with its images of deer, bears, foxes and elk, lent an authentic air to the lodge.

Her grandfather's intention when designing Beck's Wilderness Lodge was to marry two cultures: his—African-American—and his wife's—Native American. Everywhere in the lodge were reminders of the cultures: throw rugs, wooden sculptures, woven baskets and wall hangings. Three stories in height, the pinewood lodge had guest rooms on every level, plus there were cabins on the property's periphery for those who wanted more privacy.

Mina hummed as she worked. She was looking forward to taking guests on camping trips in the mountains, showing them where the fish were biting or where the rock climbing was good.

"Hello, Mina," said a deep masculine voice from behind her.

Mina instantly recognized that voice. She smiled and turned slowly so as not to lose her balance on the ladder.

Jake grinned up at her. "I have to say, you look good from this angle," he joked. "But then, you look good from every angle."

Mina laughed and climbed down. "Jake, what are you doing here?"

Jake's brain took a minivacation as his eyes feasted on her feminine curves in jeans and a T-shirt, and the way her skin seemed to glow.

He could have stood there all day, watching her, but his brain finally kicked in again, and he considered her question. When he'd gotten to Cherokee, he'd taken a room at a small motel in town. The next day the special equipment Granger had promised to send had arrived. While he was waiting for Betts's men to put in an appearance, it had occurred to him that during their information-gathering regarding the plane crash, they would inevitably find out that Benjamin Beck, who had a reputation as a mountain man in these parts, was instrumental in leading rescuers to the crash site. Therefore Jake thought he should be nearby should Betts's men decide to interrogate Benjamin Beck and his granddaughter. That's why he was here on this fine Sunday morning.

But he couldn't tell that to Mina, of course.

"The company I work for has plans to salvage the plane's cargo. I'm just waiting for the team to arrive so we can get started. In the meantime, I need a place to stay. Do you have any rooms available?"

Mina continued to smile at him. Her eyes roamed over his face. The cut on his forehead was healing nicely. He was freshly shaven. In jeans, a light jacket and a polo shirt underneath, he looked fit and healthy, vibrantly alive. The way he was looking at her made her blush, and she hadn't done that in a long time. Before she knew it she'd be giggling like an airhead, and she couldn't have that. It was undignified.

Besides, she shouldn't let herself get carried away. Even if she was wrong about his being a drug dealer, he could be a very handsome nutcase. Someone who'd fixated on her because she'd come to his rescue.

What was it he'd asked? Oh, yeah, were there any rooms available? Her heart thudded agitatedly. "We're booked up," she told him apologetically. If there was one guest in the whole world she didn't want to turn away, it was this man. Then she remembered something. "But there's a cabin left. I'm afraid it costs a bit more than a room."

"I'll take it," Jake said without hesitation.

Mina beamed at him. "All right, follow me." She looked down. "No luggage?"

"Still in the car," Jake said. "I'll get it later."

Mina stepped off the porch and Jake followed. The morning air was cool on her skin. The sky was a pale blue with a few cumulus clouds. The pungent scent of the surrounding pine forest was in the air, which, to Mina, made this day a sensual treat.

"I never did get your last name," she said to Jake as they walked toward the cabin, which sat about fifty yards from the lodge.

"It's Wolfe," said Jake. "And yours?"

"Gaines," Mina answered.

Their eyes met briefly, and Mina looked away. "Where are you from, Jake Wolfe?"

"Originally Crystal River, Florida," Jake said. "But my family moved to the Bronx, New York, when I was seven, so I consider that home, now."

"New York," said Mina, delighted she'd been right about his accent. "When we met, I thought you sounded like you were from there. I met quite a few people from New York when I was serving."

Jake nodded. "I imagine you've met people from all over the world."

"That's true," said Mina pleasantly. But she didn't want to talk about the military, so she quickly asked him another question. "You must travel a lot, too?"

Jake smiled. "A little too much for my taste," he said. "My dream is to someday own a small farm with pigs and chickens and maybe a cow or two. To

sit on the porch with my wife and bounce the grand-
kids on my knee."

Mina laughed. "You're much too young to be en-
tertaining thoughts like that. And what does a man
from the Bronx know about farm animals?"

"My grandparents owned a farm in Crystal River.
I would go there every summer. Those were the hap-
piest times of my childhood."

"Well, we don't have any cows, but we do have
horses. I can take you on a trail ride, if you like."

"I like," he said with keen interest.

Mina shook her head. "You are an enigma, Jake
Wolfe. I would never have taken you for a farm boy."

"Tell me more about you," Jake urged. "I've been
wondering why you left the army. You're so young
to have made captain. You must have been on the
fast track."

"I'll tell you someday, if you stick around long
enough," Mina promised, "but not today."

They arrived at the cabin, and Mina bent to retrieve a key that was hidden beneath a potted plant
on the porch. She saw Jake watching her with a surprised expression. "Crime is practically nonexistent
around here. But we do suggest you keep the key with
you at all times."

She unlocked the door, and they stepped inside.
Jake expected something rustic. Instead the cabin's
pine floors gleamed. The furnishings were modern and the decor tastefully done. "You have a full
kitchen," Mina said as she showed him around. "And
a full bath."

The inside air was fresh and clean. There was a flat-screen TV in the living room and a phone on the desk by the window.

"There's Wi-Fi," she told him. "And we also have laundry service. Just phone the front desk, and someone will come get your laundry and deliver it when it's done. No room service. But we do have a dining room, and we serve breakfast, lunch and dinner." She pointed to the desk and said, "A list of our amenities is on the desk, along with a TV guide and how to access our Wi-Fi. Oh, we also have a lounge, nothing special, just a place where you can kick back, have a drink and listen to the jukebox."

Jake stood still and watched her as she walked around the cabin pointing things out. He wondered if he made her nervous, or if all that pent-up energy he sensed coming off her was normal for her. "Mina," he said softly, "I want you to know I'm not a stalker or anything."

She looked startled for a second, but quickly replaced that expression with a slow smile. Her dark-brown eyes met his. "I'm not going to lie and say the possibility hadn't crossed my mind," she stated honestly. "You're still a mystery to me. But, rest assured, I'm more than capable of taking care of myself." She cocked her head, continuing to smile at him. "Okay, you're not a stalker. What are you?"

"I'm a man who's very interested in getting to know you better," Jake said. "I like you, Mina Gaines."

"That might be because I pulled you out of a downed plane," she said with a grin.

"It might be," he admitted. "Then again, it might not." He crossed the room to her. As he got closer to her, Mina's body responded to his nearness. She felt a magnetic pull toward him. Even though she still hadn't fully tossed out the idea that he was a criminal.

He reached up and gently touched her cheek. "I'm here because when we were in the mountains, I looked into your eyes and I recognized a kindred spirit. We're both lonely, aren't we, Mina?"

Mina grasped the hand that touched her cheek and squeezed it. Her emotions were so intense at that moment, her heart so full, that she didn't dare speak for fear something ridiculously sentimental would come out. How could he know how alone she felt without Keith? How desperately she wished she could go back three years in the past and change the outcome of that momentous day that had ended with him gone forever.

No, she couldn't say any of that to a man she'd known barely seventy-two hours. A man she was physically attracted to—but she wasn't yet sure what kind of man he was.

So she smiled at him and said, "I'd better get back to work."

She let his hand drop and made for the door. "You can come to the front desk and sign in at your leisure," she said in parting.

"All right, I'll do that," he said, smiling.

Mina felt his eyes on her as she left, but she didn't turn back around. That would have encouraged him further.

* * *

Mina was kept busy around the lodge the rest of the day. She did a little bit of everything, filling in when an employee failed to show up for work, doing minor repair jobs, even helping out in the kitchen.

She glimpsed Jake a couple of times during the course of the day. Once she spotted May Crowe, the young Cherokee woman who worked at the front desk, flirting outrageously with him. Jake had looked up and seen Mina, and given her a friendly wave as she passed through the lobby with a cart full of clean linen.

She'd seen him once more, in the dining room when she was helping to serve the meals. He was eating alone with his laptop open on the table. Many of the guests were either texting, talking on their cell phones or, like Jake, working on their computers while enjoying a meal.

Mina sighed as she headed back to the kitchen after serving a couple from Charleston, South Carolina, who were celebrating their fortieth wedding anniversary. Everyone was in their own world.

Jake surreptitiously watched Mina out of the corner of his eye. He wondered what he'd said to make her run away from him this morning. Admitted that he was lonely and he'd recognized the same thing in her? Had he been too presumptuous?

He'd enjoyed the sirloin steak, baked potato and garden vegetables, and now he was checking his emails. He would much rather be somewhere with

Ms. Gaines. In his profession it was sometimes hard to maintain personal relationships. He could be on assignment for months, during which he would not be in contact with a significant other. Not many women would put up with that kind of life.

He had been lucky once. Her name was Jamesa, but everybody called her Jami. They were married fresh out of college. She was a brilliant attorney, and it was his intention to work his way up to Special Agent in Charge in the DEA. They wanted children but agreed to wait five years before starting a family. He regretted that decision today, because they never made it to their fifth anniversary. Jami was killed in a car accident in their fourth year. It was Christmastime, and she was driving up to New York to be with her family. He was going to join her later. The police report said she was driving across the Brooklyn Bridge when she had to brake suddenly, hit an ice patch and spun out of control.

After Jami's death, Jake's only salvation had been work. He'd asked for the toughest assignments. He'd gotten his first undercover operation and helped bring down a Colombian drug lord. The Betts case was his second time undercover. But now, after more than five years without Jami, he was seriously craving a real life again. He wanted to be in love and go home to the same woman every night. He wanted the happiness that adoring someone more than life itself brought. Was he lonely? Damn right, he was lonely as hell.

That night he sat on the porch of the cabin where he was staying and looked up at the night sky. Out here, where there were no streetlights, it seemed the sky was somehow bigger than in the city. Tonight the velvety black canopy was graced by a huge yellow moon. Next to its illumination the stars faded into the background. The temperature had dropped a good ten degrees since sundown, and he felt the bite but was too transfixed by the sky to worry about a jacket.

"Had a nice day?" Mina asked as she strolled up. Earlier he'd seen her going into a cabin that sat several yards behind his and figured she must live there.

"One of the best days I've had in a long time," he told her truthfully. He rose and offered her his hand as she climbed the steps to the porch.

His nostrils flared at the feminine scent of her skin. She smelled freshly showered, and a faint, clean flowery aroma wafted from her. This was also the first time he'd ever seen her in a dress. She had killer legs.

After she was seated in the chair beside his, she took a deep breath and said, "I've been thinking about what you said about both of us being lonely, and I think I ought to tell you, just so you'll know—yes, I'm lonely. But it's because I'm mourning someone. I was engaged to him when he was killed in action three years ago. Since then I haven't dated anyone and, frankly, I think I've forgotten how the process works."

For a moment or two, Jake was too stunned that she would open up to him like this to say anything. His heart went out to her. He felt her pain because he'd been exactly where she was. In some ways, he was still there. He didn't think he would ever stop mourning the loss of Jami. But after five years he had learned to compartmentalize. Jami resided in a corner of his heart reserved only for her. And getting on with day-to-day living took precedence, because it was how he survived. He knew Jami wouldn't want him to fall apart because she was gone. She would want him to get as much out of life as he possibly could.

He reached out and grasped Mina's hand in his. "I know we've just met, Mina, but the dramatic way we met makes me feel as if we're already friends. Do you know what I mean?"

Mina smiled at him. "As if we've gotten the preliminaries out of the way," she said softly.

Jake was nodding his agreement. "Yes, so maybe you would feel comfortable enough to tell me about the man you loved."

Mina took a deep breath and exhaled, then for the next twenty minutes she told him all about Keith and how they had complemented each other. She could be a hothead. He was a thinker, so cool, calm and collected that his attitude had rubbed off on her, making her a better soldier and a better person.

"You said I must have been on the fast track to have made captain so young," she said softly. "You were right. My dad's an ex-army general, and my goal was to become a general someday.

"But after Keith died I lost my ambition. And when your ambition's gone, what's the point? I felt as though I was just going through the motions. So I didn't reenlist when my time was up."

"How'd you end up here?" Jake asked.

She told him how she'd spent some time back home in Raleigh with her parents and her sisters. She had four sisters. One of them was presently working in Africa. All of them were accomplished women with great careers. She was the odd one out, with no real direction. Her grandfather had suggested she come up here and give running the lodge a try. He had no one to leave the place to when he died, and she had no immediate plans for the future.

"I gave it a try and I liked it," Mina said now with a note of humor in her voice. "I've always been an active person, and this life suits me."

Jake inhaled and exhaled. The clean mountain air was invigorating. "I can see what you mean. This is the life."

Mina laughed softly. "I'm glad you like it. You know you could be in a luxurious suite at Harrah's Cherokee Casino Resort. They have over eleven hundred rooms, plus a casino and a world-class entertainment center where top country music artists perform every weekend…"

Jake leaned over and kissed her in midsentence. He let her lead him, waiting for permission to deepen the kiss. He would have been satisfied with just the taste of her lips on his tongue. After a moment, Mina sighed softly and gave herself to him. Her hand came up to caress his cheek and she leaned into him. Jake marveled at how sweet she tasted and how well the two of them anticipated each other's needs. It was a gentle kiss. It was a kiss to seal what they each knew was happening between them, a meeting of kindred souls.

When they came up for air, she heard Jake say, "Thank you for trusting me enough to confide in me. Now, let me tell you about my wife."

Mina went from mellow to ballistic in an instant. His *wife?*

Chapter 4

Jake's first clue that he had said something wrong was when Mina got to her feet, glared down at him and cried, "What? I just kissed you! You're not wearing a ring. What are you, one of those married men who take off their wedding bands whenever it suits them?"

He stood up, hands raised in a gesture of surrender. "That didn't come out the way I meant it to. I'm not married. Jami, my wife, passed away five years ago."

Mina stared up at him, mouth agape. She sat down, deflated. Jake eased back into his chair, his eyes on her face in the dim light. He hadn't bothered turning the porch light on. The only illumination came from the reading lamp in the living room of the cabin whose big picture window they were sitting in front of. He could see Mina visibly relax.

"I'm sorry," he said quietly. "What I should have said was that we have a lot in common. I lost someone I love, too."

Mina sighed softly. "All day long I debated whether or not I should be honest with you and tell you why I wasn't responding to you. Then, when I decide to take a chance on you, you mention a wife, and my first reaction is that I'd just made a fool of myself, kissing a married man."

"A bad choice of words," Jake said. "I'm an idiot."

Mina eyed him warily and leaned back in her chair. "All right, I'm listening. Please, tell me about Jami."

The tension in the air was gone. Jake smiled slowly. He told her that he and Jami were college sweethearts and had gotten married right after graduation. They'd supported each other through tough times and been grateful for the good times. It was the kind of marriage that was meant to last forever, he said. Like his parents' marriage and his grandparents'. He'd been blindsided by her death.

"She was my world," he said quietly. "For a long time I didn't know how I would go on. I didn't even care if I *did* go on. I started taking unnecessary risks, kind of testing the Reaper to see if he would come for me the way he'd come for her. More than anything, I wanted to join her."

Mina nodded knowingly. "Me, too, and having those kinds of feelings can be detrimental to others around you when you're airlifting soldiers out of a combat zone. Their lives depended on me, and all I could think about was dying."

"You were in a bad place," Jake said. "But you're past that now, right?"

She nodded. "I'm better," she said simply. "And you, how did you shake that feeling?"

Jake shrugged his broad shoulders. "Sometimes I wonder. It wasn't anything I did on purpose. It was living one day at a time without her. Plus the fact that I knew she would have kicked my ass when we met on the other side if I'd committed suicide."

"She was tough, huh?" Mina smiled.

"You remind me of her," Jake said, smiling back at her. "Not physically. She was nearly six feet tall. When it came to determination and strength of character, though, she was very tough. Like you."

"How do you know that about me?" asked Mina, her gaze meeting his.

"Not every woman would run through a forest alone to see if anyone survived a plane crash. You could have been going to a scene that would have given you nightmares for the rest of your life, yet you went anyway."

She smiled and said, "Must have been my military training kicking in."

"You know," said Jake. "If running a lodge doesn't work out for you for some reason, we're always looking for a few good people."

He couldn't believe that slip of the tongue. He was so relaxed in her presence that for a moment his guard had completely gone down. He'd forgotten he was playing a role. He was not Jake Wolfe, DEA Special Agent now. He was Jake Wolfe, mysterious businessman. He hadn't even told Mina whom he supposedly worked for.

He was relieved when Mina laughed and said, "Don't let my grandpa hear you trying to recruit me. We're joined at the hip. I'm his heir, and nothing gives him more satisfaction than knowing he's training his successor to take over his beloved lodge."

"I'm sorry. I take it back." Jake laughed right along with her. "Does that offer to take me on a trail ride still stand?"

"Yes, of course," Mina said immediately. "I'm scheduled to take a group out tomorrow morning at eight."

"I see you all like to get an early start," said Jake, stifling a yawn.

"People come here expecting to immerse themselves in nature," Mina explained. "We give them the full effect. A couple from Florida has already signed up. Meet me at the barn tomorrow morning, and wear sturdy jeans, shoes and a jacket. We provide a box lunch. Make sure you phone the kitchen early in the morning to let them know what kind of sandwich to make for you."

She rose. "It's late, I'd better go."

Jake reluctantly got to his feet. He didn't want her to go. He'd been enjoying their conversation. "I'll walk you home."

As they strolled across the expansive lawn that separated their cabins, Jake gazed up at the sky. "Being here does make you appreciate nature more. In the city I rarely look up at the sky."

"Too many big buildings in the way," said Mina. "Where do you live?"

"Atlanta." He told her the truth. He had found that the secret to maintaining an undercover life was to basically be honest about your background, altering very few details of who you were. Keeping two sets of data about two different people was difficult, and you were bound to slip up sooner or later.

"Nice town," Mina said. "My sisters and I have been there many times, mostly to concerts or sporting events."

"Oh, yeah, you said you have four sisters. No brothers?"

"No, just Lauren, Desiree and Meghan, who live in Raleigh, and Petra, who's in Africa right now."

"Oh," said Jake. "What's she doing in Africa?"

"She's a zoologist, and she's studying the great apes in Central Africa."

"That's cool," Jake said, sounding intrigued. "What do your other sisters do?"

"Lauren's an architect, Desiree's a psychologist and Meghan is a history professor."

"Your parents must be proud."

Mina smiled. "Do you have any siblings?"

"I have a brother, Leo," Jake told her. Then he laughed. "Actually, his name is Leonidas. My mother had a thing for Greek literature. I got off easy with Jason."

"Jason and the Argonauts and King Leonidas of Sparta," Mina returned easily.

"My mother would like you," Jake said.

At her door, he bent and kissed her on the cheek. "Good night, Mina. Sleep well."

"Good night, Jake," Mina softly said, and went inside.

Once she was on the other side of the door, Mina collapsed against it dramatically, giving way to the girly side of her that wanted to dance and shout that she'd just been kissed.

She was soon brought back to reality by the sound of her grandfather's voice. "Mina, is that you?"

"Yeah, Grandpa, I went for a walk before turning in."

"Did you see that fella who fell from the sky while you were out?"

"Grandpa, have you been spying on me?" Mina asked, as she walked toward the sound of his voice. She found him standing in the middle of the kitchen in his pajamas with a milk carton in one hand and a huge cookie in the other.

"You're my granddaughter," he said shamelessly. "It's my obligation to look out for you. We haven't decided whether or not he's a drug dealer, remember?"

Mina took the carton of milk from him. She poured some into a glass and handed it to him. Then she put the carton back in the refrigerator. "I don't know what he does for a living, but I don't think it's anything illegal."

"Why, because he's a good kisser?" asked Benjamin, bushy brows arched in a questioning expression. "Be careful with that one. I smell a polecat."

Mina laughed. She loved her grandfather's old-fashioned expressions. "Don't worry, I will," she assured him. She kissed his leathery cheek. "Good night, Grandpa."

With that, she turned and fairly floated on air down the hall to her bedroom.

The next morning, Mina woke in a great mood. She sang in the shower, ate a hearty breakfast and dressed, and was crossing the lawn to the lodge by seven forty-five. She went straight to the kitchen to collect the box lunches. Mabel Brown, the cook, an amply built African-American woman in her sixties, gave her a warm greeting then nodded in the direction of the two small brown bags on the counter.

"Where are the other two?" Mina asked.

"The couple from Florida isn't going because the husband is experiencing hip pain and his wife's staying with him, so they canceled their box lunch orders. Just you and the guy with the sexy voice who phoned this morning will be going on the trail ride."

Mina harrumphed, and collected the lunches along with a couple of bottles of water from the refrigerator. "These things happen. Thank you, Miss Mabel."

"You don't sound too broken up about it," Mabel said to her retreating back.

"Get your mind out of the gutter, Miss Mabel."

"Get your mind *into* the gutter," Mabel retorted with a lusty laugh.

Mina laughed as she hurried through the lobby and out the front door of the lodge. Miss Mabel had a wicked sense of humor, equal only to Mina's grandfather's, whom Miss Mabel had a major crush on. When she got to the barn, Jake was already there talking to the stable boy, Chad. Chad was a rangy kid of nineteen with dark brown skin and big, soulful brown eyes. He was very fond of Mina, and Mina of him.

"Good morning, Mina," he said, grinning at her. "I've got Cinnamon ready for you."

Cinnamon was Mina's favorite horse, an aptly named sorrel with a white star on her forehead. Cinnamon knew the trails better than her human riders, Benjamin often said. She was the oldest horse they owned and the most reliable.

"Thank you, Chad," said Mina. She smiled at Jake, who was leaning against the railing of the stall that held his mount, a dark-colored three-year-old mare by the name of Midnight. "Good morning, Jake."

Jake hadn't been able to tear his eyes off Mina since she'd walked into the barn. He'd awakened in a good mood, and now he knew why—the anticipation of seeing her again. "You look well rested, Ms. Gaines," he said, smiling.

His eyes roved appreciatively over her trim body in those tight jeans, being careful not to linger too long because he didn't want to make her feel uncomfortable. He met her eyes, and she smiled at him.

"So do you," she said. "Sleep well?"

"I did, thank you. The cabin's very comfortable."

"I'm glad to hear it," Mina said lightly.

"Chad here has been giving me some pointers on Midnight," Jake said.

"Then he's already told you she has a low tolerance for loud noises. Good going, Chad," said Mina, smiling at him.

Chad blushed and continued saddling Midnight. Finished, he led the horse out of her stall and handed the reins to Jake.

"Thank you, Chad," said Jake.

"My pleasure," said Chad. "Have a good ride."

Jake and Mina led their horses outside, and Mina turned to Jake. "I can see by the way you're handling Midnight that you're comfortable around horses," she said when they were in the bright sunshine. She stowed the sandwiches and water bottles in her saddlebags. "But I usually judge a rider on how well they mount a horse. So how experienced are you?"

Jake answered that question by climbing onto Midnight's back with practiced ease.

Mina smiled. "You don't have to show off."

Jake laughed softly. "If that's showing off, wait until you see my dismount. It's a thing of beauty."

Jake watched as Mina mounted Cinnamon and gave the signal to move out. She led the way to the adjacent woods, talking while they rode. "Grandpa likes to give the guests a history lesson and fill their heads with trivia about the flora and fauna of the mountains, but I prefer to allow the guests to ask any questions they might have about the area."

But Jake was only half listening. He was distracted by the persistent vibration of his satellite phone. The only person who had the number was Granger. Mina glanced back at him. He shrugged apologetically as he reached into his pants pocket. "Sorry, I need to get this."

He flipped open the phone as Mina turned back around and continued to allow Cinnamon to follow the trail without prodding.

"Yes?" Jake said into the receiver.

"As we speak, three of Betts's men are winging their way to your neck of the woods. I predict they'll be there in a matter of hours. Watch your back," Granger told him.

"I intend to," said Jake. "Thanks for the heads-up."

"Anytime," said Granger and rang off.

"My boss," said Jake to Mina after he'd put his phone away. "Seems the people I'm expecting to help with the salvage will be here soon."

"Oh, good," said Mina pleasantly. "I'm sure you're anxious to get started."

"Not really," Jake said under his breath. The trail widened, and he and Midnight now pulled alongside Mina and Cinnamon.

"I'm sorry, what did you say?" Mina asked.

"I said I'd rather spend time with you than go back into those mountains."

Jake smiled to himself. Truer words were never spoken. He just couldn't tell Mina the reason he preferred her company to the company of the men he was expecting to tangle with in the next few hours.

They stopped for lunch near a pristine brook. Mina got a blanket from her saddlebags, spread it out on the

ground and they sat down to enjoy the sandwiches
Mabel had made. She sat cross-legged, while Jake
stretched his legs out in front of him and groaned.
"Good Lord, woman, are you trying to kill me on
the first day? My thighs are on fire, to say nothing
of my backside."

Mina laughed, her eyes sparkling with good humor.
"I thought you were an expert rider."

Jake grinned. "I'm no expert, but I used to love to
ride when I was in my teens. I'm much older now."

"You don't look that old to me," Mina said.

"Looks can be deceiving," he returned and bit into
his ham sandwich. He chewed and swallowed. "You,
for example, look about eighteen."

Mina laughed. "Eighteen? I wouldn't be eighteen
again if somebody paid me."

"Not a good year for you?" Jake asked, smiling.

"I remember eighteen as a time when I wasn't sure
about anything. I was in military school and doing
well but not certain I should be there."

"Why weren't you certain?"

Mina's expression was contemplative. "I think I
chose the military because I wanted to please my father. He was a general, the father of five daughters,
and I was the only one who showed any signs of following in his footsteps."

"Let me guess," said Jake. "You were the tomboy
in the family? The one who always played ball with
your dad? Watched football with him?"

Mina was nodding and laughing softly. "I tried to
be the son he never had. Don't misunderstand. My

dad never encouraged me to go into the military. On the other hand, he was very proud of me when I announced that was my intention."

"Which made it harder for you to go to him and tell him you'd changed your mind?"

"Yes, it did. So I made the best of it for a while. Then I met Keith, and he gave me a fresh perspective on military life. I was actually happy flying a helicopter, knowing that we had a common goal." She looked wistful, and tears suddenly sprang to her eyes.

Jake reached over and grasped her hand. "I'm so sorry for your loss."

Mina blinked back tears. "It catches me at the oddest times, this sadness. Sometimes I feel like I'll never be normal again."

"Take it from me," Jake said softly. "The sadness never really goes away, but it does get easier as time passes."

Mina smiled at him. "Can we talk about something more upbeat? Tell me about when you were eighteen."

Jake laughed. "I was a total dweeb at eighteen."

Mina guffawed. "I find that hard to believe."

"Seriously," Jake insisted. "I was tall and gawky, wore my hair in a Mohawk, and played video games all the time. Unlike you, I didn't have any direction. My parents were worried I'd never amount to anything."

"What happened to change that?" Mina asked.

"Somehow I got into college, and that's where I met Jami and fell in love for the first time in my life. I became focused. Besides, she made it clear that she wasn't going to be with anyone who didn't believe in himself."

Mina smiled. "She sounds wonderful."

Jake grinned in response. "She wasn't perfect. But she lived life to the fullest, and when you were in her presence you felt like anything was possible."

Mina loved hearing him talk about his wife in such glowing terms. Then suddenly, something caught her attention, and she pointed behind Jake. "Shh…"

Jake slowly turned. There, not twenty feet away from them, was a doe. The deer cautiously approached the brook and began to drink from it while they watched her in awe.

They didn't speak again until the deer had finished drinking and sauntered off. "The last time I saw a deer that close was when I was visiting my grandparents' farm in Florida," Jake said quietly. His eyes met Mina's. "What other kinds of animals are out here? Are there any wolves?"

"Only you," Mina quipped.

He smiled. "Seriously, there are no wolves in the Great Smoky Mountains?"

"That depends on whom you ask," Mina explained. "A few years ago the forest service tried to reintroduce the red wolf back into the park's ecosystem, but according to them it was a complete and utter failure. But every few months someone reports a wolf sighting. So who are you to believe?"

Jake let out a very convincing howl.

Mina laughed, but she looked around to make sure

Midnight, who was skittish, was still tethered to a nearby tree. She was.

"I'm impressed."

"What boy with a name like Wolfe hasn't tried out his howl at some time or another?" Jake asked with a smile.

"You don't have any other wolfish traits I should know about, do you?" Mina asked jokingly.

Jake looked deep into her eyes. "I'm faithful like the wolf. You know they mate for life."

Mina swallowed hard. That was the sexiest thing a man had said to her in a long time.

Chapter 5

"Compared to the casino, this place is dead," grumbled Danny Betts, little brother to Charlie Betts. He was at the wheel of a late-model SUV, his green eyes scanning the slow-moving pedestrians and the generally sedate scene as he drove down Main Street in Cherokee, North Carolina.

"I disagree," said Mario Fuentes, smiling. "It's a beautiful town. Look at that mountain view!"

"Oh, I forgot," said Danny. "You probably come from a village in Mexico that looks just like this."

"You got a problem with that?" asked Mario, dark brown eyes steely.

"Gentlemen," interrupted Lonnie Duncan, the third member of their party, "can we stay focused? The point is we struck out at the casino. No one knew this Benjamin Beck guy. That article said he lived near Cherokee, didn't it?"

"Why don't you read it again?" suggested Danny.

Lonnie searched in his backpack for the article he'd printed out from a local news website. When he located it, he began reading it to himself.

"Out loud," Danny said, rolling his eyes.

"'Benjamin Beck, a local hotelier, and someone who has a reputation for being very familiar with the mountains, spotted the plane going down when he was hiking in the Great Smoky Mountains and was able to give the Army National Guard clear directions to the plane's crash site.' That's all it says about him," Lonnie said, folding the paper and returning it to his backpack.

"What's a hotelier?" Mario wondered aloud.

"Who gives a crap?" asked Danny, irritated by the whole situation. He was angry because Charlie had sent him on this chump assignment. As far as he was concerned, a trained monkey could have come to this hick town and recovered Charlie's missing goods. Once Charlie had told him he intended to get his property back, Danny had devised the plan.

Three men, one of them carrying a transponder, would locate the site and then contact a waiting helicopter that would pick up the transponder's signal and rendezvous with the men at the site, whereupon they would load the helicopter with the drugs and head home. No fuss, no muss, Danny figured. He wasn't needed here. He was supposed to be Charlie's right-hand man. He should be doing something important right now, like meeting with their Colombian connection in Miami.

"For your edification, Mario," Lonnie said, "a hotelier is someone who runs and more than likely owns a hotel." He smiled at Mario. "Good looking out, my man. This could be a clue."

He got his laptop from his backpack and, spying a café on Main Street, pointed to it and said, "Pull over, Danny. Let's see if we can get an internet connection at that café."

Five minutes later they were seated at a table in the family-owned café, imbibing coffees and chomping on freshly made cinnamon buns. Lonnie was grinning as his fingers flew over the keyboard. "Got him," he declared with satisfaction. "Benjamin Beck is the proprietor of Beck's Wilderness Lodge, which is on the outskirts of town. I was even able to find out whether they have room at the inn. They don't; they're fully booked. But that doesn't mean we can't pay him a visit, right gentlemen? Here's the address. Let's put it in the GPS and get going."

"No," said Danny. "We'll wait until dark." His green eyes glinted with malice.

"You've been unusually quiet the whole evening," Mina said as Jake walked her to her cabin that night. She stopped and gazed up at him. "What's wrong?"

They had had a wonderful day. After the trail ride Mina had other duties to attend to, but she was off the clock at dinnertime, and she and Jake had dined together and afterward taken a long walk on the grounds.

Jake sighed. He wanted to tell her everything. For the past few hours his stomach had been in knots worrying about what might go down soon. Granger might believe his theory about Betts sending men to retrieve the drugs was infallible, but Jake, who had recently seen how badly plans could go wrong, was not as confident. He'd expected Betts's men to put in an appearance anytime today. But so far there had been no sighting of any strangers on lodge grounds.

"I have no idea when I'm going to get the call to leave," Jake told her. "Which means I could be gone when you wake up in the morning, and I don't know when I'll be back this way."

"Is that what's got you tense?" Mina asked with a smile. "Look, Jake, I understand. Do what you have to do, and if or when you want to come back, you know where to find me."

Jake shook his head. "Is it that easy for you to dismiss me—us?"

"I'm not doing anything of the sort," Mina denied. "I'm being realistic. Life has taught me not to count on things turning out perfectly. Life's messy. We met, we liked each other, but if nothing more comes of it, I'm going to look back fondly on the time we had."

"Girl, you've got to raise your expectations," Jake said, then pulled her into his arms and kissed her hard. When he let go of her, Mina searched his face and breathlessly said, "Are you saying you'll definitely be back? Because I don't want to get my hopes up if you don't keep your word."

"Count on it," said Jake, holding her to his chest. "No matter what happens, I'll be back, Mina Gaines."

Nestled in his arms, Mina smiled broadly. "Then I'll be waiting."

They continued walking toward her cabin, now hand in hand. Jake looked up at the sky. There was a full moon tonight, and the sky was very clear. "Your sky is a sight to behold, Ms. Gaines. It's almost as beautiful as you are."

A little after two in the morning, Danny, Lonnie and Mario, keeping to the shadows, crept onto the front porch of Benjamin Beck's cabin. One of them picked the lock, and since the Beck cabin had no alarm, their entry was completely silent.

Earlier, while they were watching the cabin, Lonnie had argued that they were taking a risk by picking the lock. Modern homeowners protected themselves and their valuables with alarm systems. But Danny had laughed and said, "They live in paradise. People who live in paradise don't worry about burglars."

Lonnie, who'd picked the lock, now grudgingly admitted that Danny had been right. They were inside; now all they had to do was rouse Benjamin Beck without raising a ruckus loud enough to wake anyone else on the grounds of the lodge.

In her bedroom, Mina was tossing and turning, unable to settle down. She couldn't shake the feeling that Jake was involved in something illegal, even though, against her better judgment, she'd come to like him very much. He simply wasn't forthcoming enough. She still didn't know the name of the company he worked for. And she still regretted not getting a look inside one of those packages that were left on the wrecked plane. Everything didn't add up, and when things didn't add up for her, she couldn't rest.

Giving up on sleep, she got out of bed and trudged in her pajamas down the hall to the bathroom. She'd made the trip so often that she didn't bother turning on the hall light and when, out of the corner of her eye, she thought she saw a movement in the direction of the living room, she at first believed it was shadows playing tricks on her. But when she saw it again, she realized she wasn't alone in the house, and it wasn't Grandpa Beck. His eyesight was getting bad, so it was his habit at night to switch on lights in the house as he moved from room to room.

Mina pressed her back against the wall in the hallway and stood still, listening. Momentarily she heard whispering. She couldn't make out what was being said, but those were definitely human voices. Two, maybe three, people had broken into the cabin.

She couldn't imagine why anyone would want to break into her grandfather's house. But that wasn't the important thing right now, she chided herself. *First find a way to get out of this situation alive, and you can wonder why they did it later.*

She considered sneaking back into her room and

calling 911, but even if she got through it would take the police at least ten minutes to get here from Cherokee.

She and her grandfather could be dead by then. No, she had to handle this herself. And she had to handle it without alerting her grandfather as to what was happening. She didn't want him to get hurt. That would be the hard part.

Keeping her back pressed against the wall, she slowly inched her way closer to the sound of the voices. When she was around the corner from the living room, she took a quick peek and pulled back. Three males stood whispering together in front of the fireplace, one of them holding a penlight. A tall, thin one gestured for the stocky one to go in one direction and the tallest and most muscular one to go in another. The two men left the thin one, who apparently was in charge, in the living room while they went to investigate the rest of the cabin. Mina held her breath as one of them entered the hallway.

She couldn't run in either direction. If she tried to make a dash for the front door, the thin guy in the living room would stop her. If she tried to run back to her bedroom and lock her door, the one entering the hallway would see her and give chase.

So she stood still and waited for the inevitable. The guy saw her, and his eyes stretched so wide it would have been comical if it weren't so scary facing him. He was at least six-four and built like a tank. She saw instantly that he was a big, bald brother, and as soon as that thought registered, she kicked him in the groin. When he doubled over, she violently kneed him in the face. He toppled like a mighty oak, and she stepped over his prone body and ran straight for the thin guy in the living room. The stocky one had gone down the opposite hallway, where her grandfather's room was, and it was Mina's intention to disable the thin guy in the living room as quickly as possible and then go after the stocky guy before he could accost her grandfather.

By this time her adrenaline had kicked in, and Mina was in warrior mode. The thin, pockmark-faced guy must have heard the scuffle in the hallway because he turned to face her. She saw him reach for something inside his jacket, a gun in a holster perhaps, but she was on him before he could get to it. She leaped onto him and rode him to the floor, where she repeatedly bashed his head against it until he was unconscious.

She heard the guy in the hallway groaning, but she couldn't deal with him right now. She got up and ran toward her grandfather's room. Just as she was sliding to a halt at his door, the stocky one, a Hispanic guy, came out of the room with her grandfather pressed close to his body, one arm holding him by the throat and one hand holding a gun to her grandfather's head.

"We just want to talk," he said with a slight Spanish accent.

Mina observed her grandfather, who had wisely chosen not to antagonize his assailant by trying to fight him. He seemed fine.

She stood there breathing hard, eyes on the guy with the gun, ears pricked for anyone coming up behind her. "Usually when someone wants to talk they just knock on your door," she said.

The guy nodded as if agreeing with her. "Sorry," he said, "but we didn't think you'd let us in at this time of night."

"Ooh, girl, for a little bitty thing, you can pack a punch!"

Mina glanced over her shoulder and saw the black guy lumbering toward them from the hallway. She moved closer to the guy with the gun, not wanting to turn her back on him.

But the big guy wasn't interested in her when he saw the thin guy still lying on the living room floor where Mina had left him. He went to him, knelt beside him and felt for a pulse. When he found one, he slapped the guy across the face. The thin guy awakened and abruptly sat up. "Who jumped me?" he demanded.

The big guy laughed and said, "Let me shed some light on the situation." He reached over and switched on the living room light. "No need to stay in the dark now that everyone's awake, anyway." Then he pointed at Mina. "There's the wildcat who took both of us down in less than a minute."

To Mina, the thin guy was the scariest one of the bunch. While there was some humanity in the depths of the stocky guy's and the big guy's eyes, the thin one's eyes were cold and totally devoid of anything resembling compassion. His right ear was bleeding, which wasn't a surprise to Mina. She'd banged the side of his head pretty hard on the floor.

He winced as he began walking toward her, his eyes narrowed to slits. Mina knew better than to look away from his gaze. You did not take your eyes off a cobra when he was rearing up to strike.

He circled her, looking at her from all angles. "You must have already been inside when we saw the old man go in. And you weren't mentioned in the article," he said.

Mina assumed they had read about the plane crash and learned her grandfather was the one who had taken the rescuers to the crash site. That had to be why they were here—to get directions to the plane, which meant there was something valuable on that downed plane.

Mina turned with him, keeping her eyes on him. "What article?"

"The one that said the old guy led the National Guard to the crash site of the plane that went down near here."

"The guy holding my grandfather said all you wanted to do was talk," Mina said. "What do you want to talk about?"

"The location of the plane," said the green-eyed man with a smile. "We need to know it."

"And if we tell you, you'll leave us alone?" she asked.

"See, now, here's the problem with that," said Green-eyes. "We're not exactly used to the wilderness. We're city boys. We're going to need the old guy to take us to the plane. After that, we leave and never come back."

"That's going to be a problem," Mina told him. "Because my grandfather isn't the one who found the plane. I am. Grandpa led the National Guard to the site from the air. I was the one who found it on foot. So if you plan to walk in, then I'm the one you want."

"Wait a minute," Benjamin spoke up. "I'm not letting you go anywhere with these criminals!"

The stocky guy had lowered his gun arm and let go of Benjamin. Benjamin went to Mina, who put her arms around him.

They clung together while the green-eyed man continued talking. The stocky one moved near the front door and peered outside the window next to it. The big guy kept watching Mina with hungry eyes, which gave her the creeps.

"We *are* criminals," Green-eyes said menacingly, "and don't you forget it. But we are not without compassion. You'll take two of us to the plane while the other one stays here with your grandfather. After we reach the plane, I'll phone the one left behind and tell him to let your grandfather go, and you get to walk out of there unharmed."

"No," returned Mina decisively, physically putting herself between her grandfather and Green-eyes. "I lead all *three* of you to the plane. You can tie my grandfather up, but I'm not going to trust either of you alone with him. That's my final offer."

"*Your* final offer?" shouted Green-eyes, hand drawn back to strike her.

Mina didn't flinch. Her glare was as fierce as his as they began a stare down that lasted a full two minutes before Green-eyes blew air between his lips in exasperation and said, "Okay, but we leave right now."

"Fine," Mina said. "I'll get my gear."

At the sound of her acquiescence, Benjamin went berserk and yelled at Green-eyes. "What do you need my granddaughter for when one of your own men walked away from that crash? Why isn't *he* leading you into the mountains?"

Green-eyes looked at Mina, as if trying to tell her to do something about her senile grandfather. To Benjamin, he said, "You're not making sense, old man. No one survived that crash."

Benjamin angrily pointed at the big black guy. "Smaller version of him," he said. "If you don't believe me, I'll take you to him."

Green-eyes frowned. He and the other two had confused expressions on their faces. He gestured to them to join him in the middle of the room, blocking out Mina and her grandfather for a confab that included only the three of them.

Mina strained to hear what was being said.

"He's crazy," offered the big guy. "That DEA asshole couldn't have survived. We would have heard about it."

"It's possible," said the stocky guy. "Lots of people walk away from plane crashes."

"Shut up, shut up," hissed Green-eyes. "I can't think." He turned back around to face Mina.

But before he could say anything, Mina put her arm around her grandfather's shoulders and said, "Grandpa, have you been taking your meds? You know how you get when you don't take them. Remember, there were no survivors. I'm still having nightmares after seeing the condition of the bodies."

Quick on the uptake, Benjamin petulantly muttered, "There's nothing wrong with me. I don't need those pills, and you can't make me take them!"

"Now, now, don't get upset," Mina said soothingly. "I just worry about you. The doctor says those pills will help you distinguish between what's real and what's imagined."

Benjamin's lower lip trembled as though he were fighting back tears. "Is this real?" he asked Mina beseechingly. "Did three men break into our house in the middle of the night?"

"Unfortunately, yes," Mina said. "But everything's going to be all right."

She looked at Green-eyes. "Okay, let's get this show on the road. Be gentle when you tie him up. He's not well."

Mina was relieved when Green-eyes didn't offer any objections and seemed to be appeased by the performance she and her grandfather had just put on.

She looked deeply into her grandfather's eyes, hoping he could read in her expression everything she wanted to say to him: *I love you, Grandpa, and we'll get out of this alive.*

Chapter 6

Jake had no intention of sleeping. He'd gotten himself a chair and binoculars, and set up an observation post at the window of his bedroom because that window faced the Beck cabin. He'd been there for hours, moving only when he needed to refill his coffee mug.

His last email from Granger had stated that the private plane carrying the men Betts had sent to recover his property had landed over sixteen hours ago. They should have made their move by now. Even if they had recognized that this operation was the trap that it was, he felt Betts was ballsy enough to take a chance, anyway. His entire life was based on risk, after all.

Betts had a monumental ego and had been outsmarting the authorities for years. There was no reason to believe he'd lost faith in his ability to continue doing so.

Jake got up and stretched. He was wearing jeans and a T-shirt. His feet were bare. He went down the hall to the bathroom, and then strode to the kitchen to refill his coffee mug. When he got back to his post, all was quiet around the Beck cabin. For half an hour or more, nothing moved outside his window. Although he *had* noticed light seeping from behind closed blinds in the living room window a few minutes ago. He assumed someone over there was having a sleepless night, as he was. Then he saw something that made his heart race and his gut clench with anxiety. Three hulking figures, obviously male, none of them as slightly built as Mina's grandfather, were walking down the steps of the Beck cabin followed by a smaller figure, unmistakably Mina.

Cursing his stupidity, he hurriedly grabbed his jacket and pulled it on. He was already wearing his weapon in its holster. His mind was racing, as was his heartbeat. He had felt it in his gut that something was going to go down tonight, and they'd still caught him with his pants down. And now Mina was in danger.

He hadn't seen her grandfather. Had they done something to him? Jake was torn. He wanted to take off right away so that he wouldn't lose their trail. But if Benjamin Beck had been injured, he could need medical aid. He would have to go check out the cabin before pursuing the men who'd kidnapped Mina.

When he was leaving his darkened cabin, his backpack slung across his shoulder, he saw the men and Mina entering the woods. She was leading, and the men followed in single file. They all wore backpacks.

He waited a couple of minutes before running across the lawn to the Beck cabin. There were no lights on now. He stepped to the door and tried the knob. It was locked. If he broke the window next to the door to get in, there was a chance the men who'd taken Mina would hear the glass breaking. They hadn't had the chance to get out of hearing range, and sound carried farther in the dead of night.

So he had no choice but to utilize the lock-picking tools he kept on his person for such occasions. He did it quickly and quietly.

The moment he walked into the house, someone started kicking up a fuss in the kitchen, wriggling in a chair and making muffled noises that sounded as though a mouth had been covered.

Benjamin Beck's eyes narrowed when he spotted Jake coming through the door. "Mr. Beck," Jake said. "Calm down. I'll get you out of that in no time."

He made short work of the duct tape with the aid of a sharp knife. Once Benjamin was free, the older man started in on him. "She protected you!" he shouted. "She lied and told them you'd died in the crash, too. Why'd she do that? You'd better be worth it!"

At that moment, Jake didn't feel worthy of Mina's obvious faith in him. The two men stood facing each other, Benjamin Beck in his eighties and barely five-ten, Jake in excellent physical condition and in the prime of his life and six-three. But it was the bigger man who bowed to the smaller one.

Jake calmly took the beating, which he thought was well deserved. "I'm an agent with the DEA, Mr.

Beck, and I promise you, I'll find Mina and bring her back home safely."

He didn't have time to say more. He ran out of the kitchen with Benjamin waving an angry fist at him. "You'd better get her back, or I'm gonna kick your ass!"

"Watch out for snakes," Mina warned as she led the three men through the forest using a flashlight to light the way.

"Snakes!" cried the Hispanic guy, who was walking right behind her.

"Rattlers," Mina informed him. "They're nocturnal. Normally they run away from humans, but you still need to watch where you step at night. They get touchy when you step on them. But don't worry, I have a first-aid kit in my pack, and I should be able to keep you alive until someone can airlift you to a hospital."

"Danny, I didn't sign up for this," whined the Hispanic guy.

"I told you, no names," hissed the leader, whose name apparently was Danny, Mina noted.

"Oh, come on," said Mina. "We're going to be out here for hours. Can't you just give me your names?"

"I'm Lonnie," said the black guy, "and the Hispanic guy is Mario. You know Danny already."

"Under different circumstances," said Mina, "I would say pleased to meet you, but since you've kidnapped me, I'll dispense with the niceties."

"No one kidnapped you," Danny said. "You came with us of your own free will."

"I came with you because you said you'd leave us alone if I showed you the way to the plane. It was not of my own free will," Mina corrected him.

"You *assumed* that if you didn't come with us, something bad would happen to you," Danny said. "You don't know why we need your help to find the plane. Maybe our mission is entirely altruistic. Maybe there's medicine on that plane that sick kids need."

"You're right, the only evidence I have against you is *you broke into our house and threatened us*."

"You're not going to win with her, Danny," said Lonnie with a laugh. "Anyway, you already admitted we're criminals. There's no longer any need for subterfuge."

"Will you speak English?" Danny said irritably.

"No more hiding," Lonnie said. "The lady knows the score. Telling her a bunch of lies to make her feel safe while we force her to lead us into the mountains isn't working." He paused. "What's your name, sweetheart?"

"It's Mina."

"Mina, the fact is all three of us have served time in prison on some pretty violent charges. We work for one of the deadliest drug dealers in the South who has sent us to retrieve packages that were left on the plane when it went down, packages that are worth millions. Like those rattlers you mentioned a minute ago, our employer doesn't like being stepped on, and he got the worst in a deal gone bad. He's not happy about it. When he's not happy, we're not happy. Personally, I hate the woods. I'd rather be in a luxurious hotel suite with someone who looks like you."

"Since we're confessing everything," Danny said, "why don't you tell her you're a sex offender, Lonnie? She might enjoy knowing that fact."

"I've never offended any woman I've been with," Lonnie assured Mina. "Those rape charges didn't stick."

"Meaning, he got off," Danny said. "It doesn't mean the charges weren't true."

Lonnie, who was last in line and walking behind Danny, shoved him off the path. Danny fell down and rolled into a natural ditch, but he wasn't hurt and instantly got up and climbed back up, dusting dirt and leaves from his clothes as he did so. Standing in front of Lonnie, Danny said through clenched teeth, "Don't let the presence of a good-looking female make you write a check your ass can't cash. I'm in charge here, don't you forget it."

They stared each other down for some time, the moonbeams through the canopy of the forest lighting only parts of their features.

Lonnie sighed. "I never did like you."

"This isn't a popularity contest," said Danny. "You're paid to do your job, not to like me. If you don't like your job, then take off. No one's keeping you here."

"You'd like that, wouldn't you?" Lonnie accused him. "You'd like to get on the sat phone and tell Charlie that I'm a deserter. You know what he does to deserters."

"So, what's it going to be?" Danny asked. "Do your job, or die?"

Lonnie huffed and fell back in line. Danny shook his head. "I'm not turning my back on you. I'll take up the rear from now on." He directed his gaze at Mina. "Let's go."

Mina turned around and continued walking. All was quiet for the next hour or so, except for the sounds of their breathing, footfalls and the various night creatures in the forest. Mario screamed like a girl when he saw two huge eyes looking at him out of some bushes. But Mina directed the beam of the flashlight into the undergrowth and discovered a possum crouched in them. "Don't worry. He doesn't bite unless he's rabid."

Danny laughed. "I'm beginning to think you're making up things about the animals in these woods, Miss Mina."

Mina didn't deny it. "That'll teach you to interrupt *my* beauty sleep!"

Danny laughed again. "The lady has a sense of humor. Tell me, Miss Mina—are there really any dangerous animals in these woods?"

Arrrruhhhh…

The howl of a wolf sent chills down even Mina's spine. All three men were visibly startled, eyes stretched in fear, breath quickening. Mina hadn't seen faces that looked that terrified since she'd watched a cheesy horror movie.

"Madre de Dios," Mario cried, cowering behind Lonnie. "Are there wolves in this forest?"

Only one, Mina thought with satisfaction. Her gamble had paid off. Jake was on their trail.

"Wolves?" she answered, smiling. "Don't be ridiculous. There haven't been any wolves in the Great Smoky Mountains in years."

"Then what was that?" Danny cried, just as spooked as Mario.

"Maybe it was a werewolf," Mina suggested. She picked up the pace. "Please keep up, gentlemen. We have about four miles to go, and I don't want to spend any more time with you than is necessary."

"You don't have to get insulting," said Lonnie, who moved Mario out of the way and took his spot behind Mina.

Mina didn't like the fact that there was a six-foot-four sex offender right behind her. But there were more dangerous things in these woods. Like a pissed-off DEA agent.

Jake let it rip, the howl issuing from his throat with abandon. The natural acoustics of the forest magnified the sound and gave it an eerie quality. Jake knew Mina would get his signal. She was smart and resourceful. How she'd figured out that he was one of the good guys, he didn't know, but from her grandfather's rant he'd concluded that Mina had made a conscious decision to champion him.

Now he had to make sure to use the advantage of surprise that she'd given him and not screw it up, because now it wasn't only his life that was in jeopardy, hers was, too. And there was no way in hell that he was going to let anything happen to her.

The use of night-vision glasses had always been disconcerting to him. He didn't like everything bathed in green light, but it was the surest way of not being spotted should Betts's men suspect they were being followed and begin looking behind them. Jake had caught up with them fairly soon after leaving the lodge. He hung back about twenty yards, observing them. He was sometimes able to hear what was being said. He got the feeling that there was dissension in the ranks. The black guy and the white guy, whom he recognized as Charlie Betts's brother, Danny, had almost resorted to a fistfight. The Hispanic guy had given them a wide berth. Mina had stood well out of the way, which Jake was grateful for.

They were on the move again, now. Jake was really grateful for those workouts in the gym and all the jogging he'd done over the years because Miss Mina Gaines showed no mercy. Jake was close enough at one point to hear Danny Betts complain about the pace she had set and heard her say, "The weatherman predicted rain, Danny. You don't want to get caught in these mountains in a downpour unless you have shelter, which we don't. I'm going as fast as I can because I'm hoping we'll be at the plane when the rain begins. At least then we'll have some shelter."

"We're not used to walking uphill for hours," said Danny. "We have to rest."

Mina gave a sigh and relented. "Okay, you have five minutes."

The three of them sank to the forest floor, exhausted. Mina chose to remain standing and walked in place. She knew that muscles could suddenly cramp after a cessation of movement. She didn't want to be incapacitated in any way while out here with these men. If push came to shove, and she had to run for her life, she wanted to be able to.

The men drank deeply from their water bottles. Mario took a granola bar from his backpack and tore into it hungrily. "You don't pay me enough for this," he told Danny.

"You think I'm enjoying this?" Danny said. "Wait till I get back. I'm going to cuss Charlie out for this."

"Seems to me that if you were really his second in command he wouldn't have sent you on this wild-goose chase." Lonnie seemed to enjoy pointing that out, if the malicious smile on his face was any indication, Mina thought.

She took a swallow of water from her bottle and put it back. She kept her focus on the volatile men whose company had been forced on her. To say that their behavior was unpredictable would be an understatement. Admitted criminals and drug dealers with a sex offender among them, she would do well to keep her wits about her.

Knowing that Jake was following them made her feel somewhat more secure—unless there really were wolves in the Great Smoky Mountains and Jake was snug in his bed—but anything could happen before, and after, they reached the crash site.

"Stop pushing me," Danny warned Lonnie. "You don't want to make me angry."

"What are you, the Incredible Hulk?" Lonnie said with a derisive laugh.

Danny launched himself at Lonnie, and because Danny was strong and wiry Lonnie couldn't get him off of him, even though he outweighed him by a hundred pounds. Danny had gone crazy, throwing a barrage of punches at Lonnie's face, and at one point tried to bite his ear off.

Mario pulled Danny off Lonnie and wrapped his arms firmly around him until the madness had subsided. "Let's calm down, fellas. I know we're out of our element, here, but we can do this if we work together. Charlie must have had a reason for putting the three of us together."

His words made Danny think. Maybe his brother actually did have a reason for sending him to North Carolina with Mario and Lonnie. Maybe Charlie was setting him up to take the fall. Paranoia had set in, and he didn't trust anyone anymore. He looked around at Mario and Lonnie, who was pressing his hand to his bleeding ear. *That's two bleeding ears tonight,* Danny thought with a smirk.

His gaze fell on the girl. She was the only calm one among them. Maybe she was too calm. Maybe she was leading them in circles. But what reason would she have for doing that? She was alone in the woods with three violent men who could rape and murder her and bury her body where no one would ever find it. It was to her advantage to cooperate with them. Although he certainly had no intention of honoring his word and actually letting her walk out of here once she'd led them to the plane. He would be an idiot to do that, and Danny Betts was no idiot.

"We've had enough rest," he said sharply to Mina. "Let's move."

Mina was more than happy to continue their trek. It seemed that whenever there was a lull in the walking, a fight broke out among them.

She couldn't guess what Jake's plan to apprehend the men entailed, but after hours of walking she was beginning to think he was waiting until they reached the crash site to make his move.

She sighed deeply as she adjusted her backpack and began moving south. They had passed the tree she'd climbed in order to get the lay of the land on the day of the crash some time ago. They had only about an hour left of uphill climbing.

Chapter 7

They soon got into a rhythm. Mina led the way, followed by Lonnie, then Mario and Danny. When they were almost at their destination, Mario asked them to stop for a few minutes while he went to relieve himself.

"Okay, but make it quick," Danny grumbled, and sat down with his back against a tree trunk well away from Lonnie, whom he was still shooting angry glances at.

Mario hurried off and Lonnie sat down, ignoring Danny, and gestured for Mina to take a seat beside him underneath a sugar maple tree.

Mina shook her head. "I prefer to stand, thanks."

Lonnie looked up at her. "Where'd you learn to fight like that?" he asked. "You were on me before I could react."

"Over twenty years of martial arts. Our dad started all of us in classes when we turned seven. And I'm ex-army."

"Me, too," Lonnie said, sounding excited that they had something in common.

Mina didn't comment, and Lonnie must have taken her silence as judgment because he added, "You're wondering how I ended up a criminal, right?"

"I'm not wondering anything about you," Mina said softly. "Maybe *you've* got something to feel guilty about."

Scowling, Lonnie rose. "Oh, I've got a long list of things to feel guilty about, and you're gonna make it on that list if you're not careful."

Danny, as quick as lightning, came up behind Lonnie and put the barrel of his pistol next to his ear. "Don't threaten the wilderness guide, Lonnie. That's bad form."

Lonnie instinctively reached into his jacket to get his own weapon, but soon found out it was no longer in its holster.

"I took it when I jumped you a few minutes ago," Danny told him. "Hid it in my jacket and threw it away at the first opportunity. You're behaving erratically, Lonnie boy, and I can't have you going off the deep end with a Glock in your hand."

To Mina's surprise, Lonnie didn't get angry. He stood looking at Danny and shaking his head in disgust. "This is some crap assignment!"

"You said it," Danny agreed with a smile. "Now, let's try to keep our heads. No more threatening Miss

Mina. And when we get back home, I'll put in a good word for you with the boss. It's understandable that we would not react well to a situation so radically different from what we're used to. Charlie will get that. No harm, no foul."

Lonnie turned away, his huge chest heaving, the only sign that he was agitated.

Danny cautiously put his gun back in its holster.

A couple of minutes later Mario jauntily bounced back through the bushes and declared, "Okay, let's go."

"Move out, Miss Mina," Danny ordered. And Mina did as she was told.

Lonnie wasn't the only one agitated. Jake was getting more concerned for Mina's safety by the second and was seriously thinking of getting the drop on the men before they reached the plane. Granger wanted him to catch them with the merchandise, but Granger wasn't out here watching an innocent woman go through the emotional abuse Mina was taking. The men were hostile with each other. How long would it be before they turned on her?

Reasonably he knew they were counting on her to lead them to the plane and probably wouldn't do anything to prevent that from happening. Danny Betts had proven that when he'd jumped between the black guy and Mina a minute ago.

Jake wanted this over with. It had been absolute torture watching Mina's face when that gun had come out. It seemed that she had realized she was at the mercy of madmen.

* * *

Mina walked as though her life depended on her reaching the plane as soon as possible. Daylight had come a couple of hours ago. The mountain air was cool, and fog hung in it and got thicker as they ascended. She felt weak with relief when she spied the wrecked plane. She didn't speak but stood still on the trail and pointed to it.

Danny came around her. "Good job, wilderness guide," he said with a grin. "Now you can relax. We'll take it from here."

There was a huge boulder nearby, and Mina went and sat down. She had no desire to accompany them to the plane. She was hoping Jake would appear soon and take them down, and she planned on being well out of the line of fire when he did.

"Yeah." Mario complimented her as he followed Danny. "Good job, Mina."

Lonnie just gave her an angry glance and grunted at her when he walked past. Apparently his feelings were still hurt because she hadn't jumped up and down with happiness when he had told her he was also ex-army.

Mina smiled at him. "Aren't you glad this is almost over?"

"Sugar, it's not over yet," he said ominously and kept walking.

Mina watched them approach the plane. The National Guard had sealed it as best they could after rescuing Jake and removing John Monahan's body. Now Danny was having a hard time opening the plane's door. He gestured for Lonnie to give it a try. The big man opened it on the first try. Then the three men disappeared inside.

Mina looked around and heard a low voice say, "Mina!"

Jake! She started to turn in the direction of his voice, but he hurriedly said, "Don't turn around. Listen, I want you to hide in the woods. And don't come out until I call you. Understand?"

Mina nodded.

"Go!" he urged, his voice raspy with emotion.

Mina desperately wanted to see him. She was so relieved that she'd been right about him that she felt as if a heavy weight had been lifted from her heart. Stress relief in the form of tears ran down her cheeks as she ran back into the forest.

Inside the plane, Danny was checking one of the marijuana bundles. The plane was open to the elements due to its windshield being broken out. But there had obviously been no rain recently. The inside was moist with morning dew; however, it was not nearly as damp as it would have been after a downpour. He finally got the bundle open. The product was dry and in as good shape as it had been when it had been packaged. Charlie would be pleased.

Mario reached in and grabbed a handful of the dried leaves. "This looks better than I thought it would, coming from Canada," he commented.

"Mexico isn't the only place you can find good pot," Lonnie said, coming around to stick his hand in.

Danny gave him a dark look. "Nobody's watching the girl?"

Lonnie narrowed his eyes at him. "You didn't tell me to watch her."

"Do I have to tell you everything?" he yelled. He nodded toward the exit. "Go make sure she's still there."

Lonnie's chest was doing that agitated thing again. Danny was sure that if he hadn't thrown his gun away, Lonnie would have shot him.

"I'll go," Mario volunteered.

"I want him to go," Danny said.

"I'm tired of you treating me like your personal slave," Lonnie warned.

Danny smiled coolly. "I'm tired of you, period."

"Come on, then," Lonnie challenged him. "Let's take this outside. No guns, just fists."

Danny sighed. "I don't have time for this foolishness." He took his gun out and shot Lonnie point-blank in the head.

Lonnie was dead before he hit the padded roof of the upside-down plane.

Mario screamed with his hands over his ears. The sound of the gun's report in the close quarters of the plane reverberated painfully in his head. "Why'd you do that, man?"

"Because he was just waiting to stab me in the back, that's why," Danny said reasonably. He stepped over Lonnie's body. "Now, go make sure the girl's still there. I don't know why I didn't just shoot her as soon as we got here."

Fearing for his life, Mario hurried to follow Danny's orders. When he got outside, he saw at once that Mina was no longer where they'd left her. He looked back at the plane, then at the boulder where he'd last seen Mina. Indecision ate at his insides. If he went back and told Danny that Mina was gone, Danny might shoot him out of spite. He looked longingly at the forest. The overnight hike had been hell, but re-entering the forest was preferable to dying. He ran toward the forest.

Unfortunately, he didn't get far. Jake stepped into his path as soon as he reached the tree line. Mario let out a frightened, keening sound because it appeared as if Jake had materialized out of nowhere. Then his mind seemed to recognize that, indeed, there was a man standing in front of him, and he went for his gun. It was the last thing he was conscious of doing before Jake punched his lights out.

Jake dragged the body into the forest, where he turned his prisoner over onto his belly, handcuffed his hands behind his back and took off the unconscious man's belt, wrapping it around his ankles, thereby hobbling him. "Sleep well," Jake said before rising and walking purposefully toward the plane. There were two of them left. He'd already called for backup, and the helicopter carrying the agents would arrive soon.

Jake approached the plane cautiously, his weapon drawn. He knew from months of being in close proximity with Danny Betts that he had a volatile temper.

He'd already heard the sound of gunfire. And the terrified look on that guy's face as he was running for the woods told him that whatever he was about to face in the downed plane wasn't going to be pretty.

He focused, his ears pricked for any warning sounds from within. Keeping his back to the side of the plane, he slowly inched his way to the door, which was hanging open.

Staying low, he peeked around the corner and saw Danny trying to get a signal on a cell phone.

Quickly rising into a shooter's stance and blocking the doorway, Jake shouted, "No sudden moves, Danny!"

Danny let the phone he was holding fall to the ground and smiled at Jake. "I was told *you* were dead."

"Your brother gave it his best shot," Jake said dryly. His gaze fell on Lonnie's body. "I wondered which of you would wind up dead. Now I know."

"He was an asshole," said Danny. He met Jake's eyes. "You do realize this is a setup? My brother is playing both of us for fools. It was a perfect solution for him. He gets rid of me and throws the Drug Enforcement Administration a bone."

"Why would he throw his own brother under the bus?" asked Jake curiously.

"Because I'm ambitious," Danny told him. "I've been complaining about his not giving me enough responsibility, and he believes I'll eventually kill him and take over."

"Would you?"

"Probably," Danny said. "I see no reason to lie."

Suddenly the sound of a chopper's blades pierced the tranquil silence of the mountain ridge. Neither man in the downed plane allowed the interruption to distract him. Jake kept a close watch on Danny. Danny's eyes never left Jake's face.

"How this plays out," Jake said slowly, "depends on you, Danny. Are you going to let Charlie get away with this? You know he's more than capable of framing you and making it look like you're the one behind the organization. But if you testify against him, he'll go to prison."

"But I'll go to prison, too," Danny said. He glanced down at Lonnie's body. "That wasn't self-defense. He wasn't armed."

The tension in the body of the plane was palpable. Neither Jake nor Danny Betts felt in control. Jake wanted to take Danny alive so that the agency could finally build a case against Charlie Betts and prosecute him to the full extent of the law.

Plus, he couldn't be sure the sound of the chopper meant that *his* backup had arrived. Maybe *Danny's* people had gotten here first. There was no way three men would have been able to carry all the bundles out of here on foot, so it stood to reason they'd arranged to have a chopper follow a signal to their location. And he was also under pressure because there was a woman he cared about somewhere out there who was depending on him to make it out alive and make sure she got back home safely. She'd been let down by life enough. He didn't want to add to her disappointment.

* * *

Danny considered his options. Personally, he didn't believe he had any way out of the mess he was in. All scenarios were bad. He could take his chances and pull his gun on Jake and succeed, or get killed. He could testify against Charlie and get a lesser sentence for his cooperation, but he'd still go to prison, and in prison he would be a sitting duck. Charlie would pay someone to kill him out of spite. No one double-crossed Charlie Betts and lived to tell the tale. Look at this plane he was standing in right now. It had been the death place of someone who'd tried to double-cross Charlie Betts, and he had wound up very dead.

Resigned to his fate, he smiled at Jake and said, "Tell Charlie I went out like a man." Then he reached for his gun.

When Danny went for his weapon, Jake did what he was trained to do. The bullet pierced Danny's heart. He died instantly and fell right beside Lonnie's body, his arm splayed across Lonnie's chest.

Outside, Mina heard the gunshot, and her heart fell to the pit of her stomach. Her eyes were glued on the plane as she willed Jake to walk out of it unhurt and victorious.

Long minutes passed during which she was in agony, worried that Danny or one of the other men had killed Jake.

She ignored the helicopter. It was another Black Hawk with an Army National Guard emblem on its side. She saw it land in her peripheral vision, her gaze still riveted on the plane's door.

At last, Jake emerged from the plane, gun at his side. He waved to the occupants of the helicopter, possibly signaling that all was well and he had everything under control.

After that he began running toward the woods, shouting, "Mina, Mina, it's safe to come out now!"

That's all Mina needed to hear. She came out of her hiding place, and when Jake saw her he let out a whoop, put the safety on his weapon, returned it to its holster inside his jacket and continued running toward her.

They were both breathless when they met midway between the tree line and the crash site and hugged tightly. Jake spun her around. "Thank God you're all right."

When he set her down, he peered into her upturned face, a wide grin on his own. "I could kiss you!"

"Nobody's stopping you," said Mina, her heartbeat doing double-time.

They kissed like lovers who'd just been reunited after a long time apart, hungrily and passionately. Time stood still as they stood there, clinging to each other, their mouths giving and taking pleasure of the sweetest kind.

It was with reluctance that they eventually parted and lovingly looked into each other's eyes. The first words out of Jake's mouth after that display of affection were, "I'm sorry I couldn't tell you the truth."

His big hand cupped her face. In spite of everything she'd been through in the past eight hours, her eyes glowed as she looked up at him. "Don't worry about it," she said. "You were doing your job. I understand duty." She laughed shortly. "When you tried to recruit me, you were talking about the DEA, weren't you?"

He grinned. "Yeah," he admitted. "Have you changed your mind about joining up?" He turned them around, and they began walking toward the helicopter that had touched down nearby.

"No, thank you," said Mina. "I've had enough excitement to last me a lifetime. I'm very happy at the lodge."

"Speaking of the lodge," Jake said, reaching into his jacket pocket for his sat phone, "Call your grandfather, please! The last time I saw him he was vowing to kick my ass if I didn't bring you back safe and sound."

Laughing, Mina took the phone. "Yeah, that's my grandpa."

Chapter 8

"You might just as well throw me off the mountain," Mario said as Jake escorted him to the Black Hawk a few minutes later. "I'm as dead as Danny and Lonnie. Danny shot him in cold blood, by the way. Lonnie got on his nerves one time too many. It's a damn shame because, as dudes go, Lonnie wasn't a bad dude."

"You seem to like talking," Jake said. "Why don't you save it for the interrogators?"

Mario shook his head sadly as he climbed into the Black Hawk. "It doesn't matter what I say, it won't end well for me."

"Look, buddy," Jake said, "I'm not going to lie to you. You're in deep trouble. Danny believed that Charlie set him up, which means he sent him up here because he knew we would be waiting. By his actions I can only conclude that you, Danny and the guy you call Lonnie were expendable as far as Charlie Betts was concerned. Are you going to take that lying down, or are you going to make him pay for setting you up? The choice is yours."

Mario went to say something, but Jake silenced him with a raised hand. "Don't say anything else. There's no point. If you decide to cooperate, you'd just have to repeat everything later." Jake left after saying that.

Before Jake and Mina boarded the Black Hawk, Jake pulled her aside. "Just so you won't be in the dark about what went down here, the man I had to kill, Danny Betts, was the brother of a drug dealer we've been trying to take down for three years now. And, Mina, we can't drop you off at the lodge like last time. Because you were kidnapped, you'll have to make a statement. I'm sorry. You've already been through hell, and you must be exhausted. I'll ask them to make the process as quick and painless as possible. But you're going to have to go to Asheville with us. I promise I won't leave your side until it's over."

Mina let out a tired sigh as she looked into his eyes. "All right," she said resignedly. All she wanted to do was go home, take a hot shower, eat some comfort food and go to bed, in that order.

Jake hugged her, not caring that they had an audience. "It'll be over soon, and then I'll drive you back to Cherokee."

Mina mentally corrected her wish list. She wanted to go to bed, yes, but maybe not alone.

"You must be getting tired of Cherokee," she joked.

"On the contrary, I'm very fond of Cherokee," Jake said as he led her to the Black Hawk. "It has the world-famous Beck Wilderness Lodge and very beautiful views." The way he was gazing down at her, as if at that moment she mattered more to him than anything else in the world, told her she was his favorite view by far.

In Asheville, Mina tolerated the routine medical examination at Mission Hospital. The doctor said that, aside from being a little dehydrated, she was in excellent health. After that the local police escorted her to the police station, and the chief of police and one of his detectives commenced interviewing her about her ordeal.

An hour later two FBI agents arrived and presumed to take over the interview, whereupon Jake took them outside for a private consultation, after which Mina never saw them again. She suspected there was a long-standing rivalry between the FBI and the DEA when it came to high-profile cases. Everyone wanted the credit for the bust. The satisfied expression on Jake's face when he returned to the room told her the DEA had won that round.

In fact, when Jake returned to the room in which Mina sat on one side of a table and the chief of police and the detective on the other, he must have still been in a fighting mood. When the chief, a balding man with a huge belly that lapped over his thick belt, asked Mina a question she had already answered twice, Jake blew up and said, "That's enough. I'm taking Ms. Gaines someplace where she can rest and recuperate. If you want to know anything else, you have her address in Cherokee."

Mina smiled for the first time in hours as she slowly got to her feet.

"What gives you the authority to do that?" the chief blustered as he stepped around the table to face Jake. Mina thought he might actually bump Jake with his belly, he was so angry.

Jake whipped out his badge and showed it to the chief. "You obviously weren't listening when I said I was DEA. Maybe this'll help," he said calmly.

He reached for Mina's hand. "Ms. Gaines, if I may?"

Mina gave him her hand with a contented sigh. "Thank you, Special Agent Wolfe."

The chief got red in the face but didn't get in their way. He stood helplessly aside, muttering expletives under his breath. The detective, a muscular young guy, looked primed to pounce as soon as he got the go-ahead from the chief. Mina could see the eagerness in his blue eyes.

But to her relief, the chief never gave it.

There was an SUV waiting for Jake and Mina when they got outside. Jake held the door for Mina. After she climbed in, he went around to the opposite side and got in the backseat with her. "Take us to the Renaissance, please?" he politely asked the young male agent at the wheel of the vehicle. "It's at 31 Woodfin Street."

After they were under way, Jake explained, "It's already getting dark. We'll stay here tonight, and I'll drive you back to Cherokee in the morning."

Mina didn't protest. She was bone weary, so tired that her emotions were close to the surface, and she felt like crying with relief. She closed her eyes, leaned back on the cushy leather seat of the SUV and said, "A hot bath and a meal would be good."

At the Renaissance, Jake instructed the agent behind the wheel of the SUV to wait for him while he escorted Mina upstairs.

Mina walked into the luxurious lobby in her dingy clothes and suddenly felt very out of place. She was happy that they didn't need to stop at the desk and register.

"The agency has taken care of everything," Jake told her. At the bank of elevators he pressed the up button, and on the third floor he produced a key card from his inside jacket pocket and unlocked a room door.

"To give you a little privacy, I'll go get us some food," he said, not even going inside. "Is there anything you're allergic to that I should know about?"

"Nothing," Mina said softly, figuring they had shared meals and he knew she had a hearty appetite. Besides, she was so hungry that she would have eaten anything he brought her, as long as it was already dead and cooked.

"Good, then go take a relaxing bath, and I'll be back before you know it," Jake said.

He left, closing and locking the door behind him. Mina walked farther into the elegantly appointed room and began peeling off her clothing. In her backpack she invariably kept a change of clothing and her toothbrush and toothpaste. She removed the clothing and unrolled the individual items atop the bed. After that, she went into the large bathroom that had a huge bathtub and began running water into the tub. Then, thinking better of it, she changed her mind and took a shower, instead. She was so exhausted, she didn't want to risk falling asleep in the tub.

When Jake got back with the food, a sumptuous meal for two from the hotel's bistro, Mina was asleep in one of the room's queen-size beds, wearing the fluffy white robe the hotel provided.

He set the food on the table next to the window. She looked so peaceful he didn't have the heart to wake her. He took the opportunity to shower in the connecting room the agency had provided for him.

He was brushing his teeth in the bathroom after his shower and caught his reflection in the mirror. He still had wide-set golden-brown eyes, a square jaw that needed a shave right now, a full mouth and a nose that was too long in his estimation, and he still thought the fact that it'd once been broken in a fight gave it character.

No, nothing had changed about his face. But the man looking back at him was a changed man. He'd killed someone today, and even if that man would have killed him if he hadn't defended himself, he nonetheless felt bad about it. He'd never killed anyone before. There was something sacred about the human spirit to him. It was not his to take. He felt empty inside and knew he'd feel that way for the rest of his life. The sensation might lessen as time passed, but it would always be there.

He pulled on the robe that matched Mina's and went across to her room to check on her. She'd turned to her other side, probably getting more comfortable, and was still sleeping soundly. He went to the desk and wrote her a quick note: *Mina, I'm leaving the door open between our rooms so I can hear you should you need me. Jake.*

He left the note on the nightstand so she would see it when she awakened. He glanced in the direction of the food before he turned and headed for his bed because he was more tired than he was hungry. He was asleep less than a minute after his head hit the pillow.

When Mina woke up, the lights in the room were dim and there was a delightful aroma in the air. Food! She sat up in bed, stretched and got to her feet. Then she saw the note Jake had left and read it. She smiled and put it back on the nightstand.

Padding barefoot over to the table that held the tray of food, she lifted the coverings and discovered enough food for two people—broiled chicken, new potatoes, sautéed green beans with slivers of almonds, dinner rolls with real butter on the side and iced tea in two tall glasses.

Her stomach growled in anticipation as she sat down and began to eat. As was usually the case when she'd physically overdone it, she began to feel full after devouring only a small portion of the food and put down her fork. She was thirsty more than anything else and finished the tea.

She looked down at her robe. She wasn't wearing anything under it, and she had no nightgown or pajamas to change into. She would have to sleep in a T-shirt and panties tonight.

She was debating whether or not to change into her fresh clothes, since she didn't believe she'd be going to sleep again for a while, when Jake cleared his throat.

"May I come in?" he asked from the doorway.

"Please do," Mina said pleasantly. She got up as he entered the room. She saw that he was wearing jeans and a sleeveless T-shirt but was barefoot.

She put her hand to her throat. "I should get dressed."

Jake smiled at her. "Mina, you're perfectly decent. But if you'd feel more comfortable, I'll wait until you've changed."

"No," she told him. "You must be starving. Please eat. I'll go into the bathroom to change. Sit, enjoy yourself. The food's delicious."

Jake glanced at her practically untouched meal. "You weren't hungry, huh?"

"My stomach's funny when I'm overly tired. I'll be back to normal by tomorrow."

Jake sat down at the table and began eating. He watched her as she gathered her fresh clothes and made a beeline for the adjacent bathroom. "Stress probably has something to do with it, too," he said. "How're you feeling?"

"Three men have died around me in less than a week," Mina called to him while she changed. "I'm having flashbacks of Afghanistan, to tell you the truth. How're *you* holding up?"

Jake didn't immediately answer, and Mina didn't expect him to. She finished dressing and walked back into the room wearing jeans and a black T-shirt. She'd tied her braids back in a ponytail, and she was still barefoot.

She picked up the remote and aimed it at the flat-screen TV in the armoire. "I wonder what's on HBO," she murmured absentmindedly.

From across the room, Jake smiled at her attempt to appear nonchalant after asking him how he was doing after killing a man. She hadn't used those words, but he was sure it was what she'd been wondering when she'd asked him how he was holding up. The things they had in common, military service, facing life or death situations, all made it unnecessary for them to walk on eggshells around each other. She felt confident enough to ask the hard questions, and that was all right with him.

At that moment, though, he simply didn't trust himself to be able to choose the right words that would explain how he was feeling after taking a human life.

Therefore, he consumed the meal in front of him and postponed the conversation. He knew Mina would understand that.

When he'd finished eating, Mina was sitting on the couch with her feet curled up under her, watching the evening news on a local channel. He went and sat down beside her and put his arm around her shoulders. She scooted closer and laid her head on his shoulder. They both sighed contentedly, as if this was what they'd been waiting for all day, this moment of quiet in a safe cocoon made for two.

They didn't say anything for a few minutes, just watched the news, which was the usual horror show of murders, terrorist acts and dire warnings about the economy.

Then Jake picked up the remote and turned the TV off.

"In my ten years as an agent, I've used my weapon only two other times, and no one ended up dead either time. I guess I've been lucky. Danny Betts wasn't going to be taken alive. He didn't want to face prison, and he definitely didn't want to face his brother. I had no other option. Even knowing that I didn't have a choice, I still regret firing the gun that robbed a man of his life."

Mina took his hand and squeezed it reassuringly. "He was mean as a snake," she said. "I looked into his eyes, and they were vacant, soulless. Danny Betts was a scary man. Lonnie and Mario were innocent babes compared to him. I don't know what happened to make Danny the way he was, but it must have been something awful."

Jake hugged her close and said, "From what I gathered when I was undercover, his brother Charlie had him dealing on the streets of Atlanta when he was barely out of elementary school. He was managing the methamphetamine side of the business in the backwoods of Georgia in his twenties, associating with the most reprehensible drug dealers you can imagine. Yes, he has seen some horrible things. But worst of all is the fact that he was used and tossed aside by his own brother. Danny might have been soulless, but Charlie Betts is the devil."

"Sounds like you really want to take him down," Mina said, her eyes searching his.

"We've been trying, but he always manages to slip through our fingers," Jake told her.

He was having a hard time concentrating on work when Mina was so close. Looking into her rich dark-chocolate eyes, which were looking back at him with such implicit trust, made him feel all warm inside.

The golden-brown tone of her flawless skin and her signature scent, which was wafting off her and assailing his senses with intensity, all worked to confound his attempts at staying aloof. He was weak for her, and he knew he *had* to resist because this was not the time for a seduction. She was officially in his custody until he took her back to Cherokee. It was his duty to make sure she was safe and sound, and protected from anyone wishing her harm.

* * *

Mina felt the pull of Jake's sexual magnetism. He was all male, from his muscular body to his well-shaped feet. She appreciated a man who took care of himself.

She was trying to stifle the desire that was building inside of her. She knew Jake had a job to do, and she honestly didn't want to make it more difficult for him to do it. She understood that nothing of a sexual nature could happen here tonight. There must be some kind of rule against that kind of behavior between a DEA agent and the victim of a crime perpetrated by someone the agency was investigating. She didn't know the technical term for it, though.

She looked deeply into Jake's eyes. Perhaps she should just ask him. "You and I," she began. "If we, um, got together, would it be against agency rules?"

Jake's smoldering golden-brown eyes raked over her face. He desperately wanted to kiss her breathless, just devour that luscious mouth of hers. "I can't think of one," he said, and bent and planted a kiss on her that had her up and onto her knees, pressing him into the couch until he was flat on his back and her body was straddling his and writhing with pleasure.

"Mina, Mina," Jake said between kisses. "We can't do this."

"Do what?" Mina breathed. She sighed and the kissing resumed, this time with even more intensity than before. By the time they came up for air again, Jake was the one on top.

Mina felt his erection, which was quite insistent,

she thought, on her belly, and her hand went, of its own accord it seemed, to caress it. Jake shot her a warning look. "You're not playing fair."

"I'm not playing," Mina told him frankly.

"You're vulnerable right now, Mina."

"So are you."

"I don't have any condoms."

Mina went still. She looked into his eyes, her expression disbelieving. "Seriously?"

"I wasn't planning on seducing you."

From underneath him on the couch, Mina gestured for him to get off her, and they sat up.

Smiling at him regretfully, Mina said, "I guess this wasn't meant to be."

"It's for the best," Jake said. "You could be suffering from trauma and you're just not aware of it. I'm not in the best mental state right now, myself. I want our first time to be perfect and for all the right reasons."

Mina was nodding in agreement. She couldn't bring herself to tell him, but somewhere in the back of her mind her conscience was warring with her libido. While her body was telling her she wanted to make love to Jake, her heart was saying it would feel as if she were cheating on Keith.

She bent forward and got the TV's remote from the coffee table in front of the couch. She channel surfed until she found a familiar film on the screen. Her eyes lit up. *"Star Wars,"* she cried. "The good one."

Jake sat back and put his feet up on the coffee table. "You mean the first one."

She grinned at him. "Exactly."

"You're a woman after my own heart," Jake said, as he put his arm around her and pulled her close. They settled down to watch.

On the screen Luke Skywalker was piloting his spacecraft around enemy craft in an attempt to target the Empire's space station. Moments later, his character uttered Mina's favorite line in the film. Both she and Jake yelled the line with Luke Skywalker: "Just like Beggar's Canyon back home!"

They looked at each other and burst out laughing.

"That's why I became a pilot," Mina said through her laughter.

She looked at Jake, how his eyes sparkled with humor, his grin so infectious. From the beginning he had been a source of curiosity for her. Even when she hadn't trusted him, she'd been attracted to him. Now that she knew what he'd been hiding, she felt somehow vindicated. Her instincts hadn't been that far off the mark.

She settled back in his arms and laid her head on his shoulder. "This is the most relaxed I've been in a while," she murmured.

"Me, too," Jake said softly as he affectionately tightened his hold.

Chapter 9

"Oh, my God, I recognize that Hummer," Mina cried the next day as she and Jake drove onto the lodge's property. It had taken them only about an hour to get to Cherokee from Asheville. Now Mina was staring at the black Hummer.

Jake pulled the SUV behind the Hummer on the lawn in front of the cabin Mina shared with her grandfather. "Whose is it?" he asked casually.

"My father's," Mina said, reaching for the door's handle. "I asked Grandpa not to tell my parents anything until I got home. Their being here can't be a coincidence. Raleigh's nearly five hours away."

Jake reached for his door's handle, too. "Give him the benefit of the doubt. Maybe your family just wanted to surprise you."

Jake could be right—not about her folks wanting to surprise her, but about there being more relatives besides her dad here for a visit. He probably brought her mother and possibly one or all three of her sisters with him.

Mina looked at Jake. "Brace yourself, you're about to meet my family, and they're not cute and cuddly like Grandpa."

"I can't wait," said Jake optimistically.

"Try to hang onto that attitude," Mina said ominously.

"They're here!" they heard a female voice screech. Mina's youngest sister, Meghan, came bounding down the front steps of the cabin and running to meet her. Mina was enveloped in her arms in seconds.

"M, are you all right? We were so worried," Meghan whispered in her ear.

"I'm fine, sis, really. I'll fill you in later, all right?"

Mina looked over Meghan's shoulder and saw her entire family spilling out of the cabin: her father, ex-army general Alfonse "Fonzi" Gaines, her mother, Virginia Beck Gaines, and the other two of her sisters who still lived in Raleigh, North Carolina: Lauren and Desiree.

Her grandfather walked onto the porch but didn't venture down the steps into the yard.

Mina was grinning by the time she'd been hugged by everyone.

Mina grasped Jake by the arm and pulled him forward.

"Everyone, this is DEA Special Agent Jason Wolfe," Mina introduced him. "Jake, this is my family."

"Good to meet you, young man!" boomed the general, coming to vigorously pump Jake's hand. "I'm Mina's father, Alfonse."

Jake smiled at the tall, dark-skinned and well-built ex-army general who, with his bald head, made Jake think of Samuel L. Jackson.

"It's a pleasure, sir," Jake said politely, smiling.

Then the general presented his wife. Jake gazed into the upturned face of the beautiful, petite woman, a woman whom he could see Mina got her looks from. They had the same golden-brown skin, abundant, wavy black hair—although Mrs. Gaines's was liberally laced with silver—and dark brown eyes. He felt those sharp eyes assessing him as she shook his hand. He hoped he measured up in her estimation. But he was determined not to let it bother him if he didn't.

"My wife, Virginia," Alfonse Gaines said with pride.

Crinkles appeared around her eyes as Virginia Gaines smiled up at him. "My daughters have a penchant for rescuing handsome men," she said in a well-modulated voice.

Jake didn't know what to make of that statement, so he simply said, "Mrs. Gaines, I can see where Mina gets her good looks."

Virginia beamed at him. "A man who knows how to compliment a woman," she murmured in approval. "I like that."

She followed her husband's example and, in turn,

introduced him to Mina's sisters, one lovely woman after another.

Meghan was the one who'd come running out of the cabin. She was a little taller than Mina and perhaps a bit younger, too. All of the sisters were dressed casually, but they had a polished appearance, as though they rarely left the house without being made up and appropriately dressed. Charming and gorgeous was how he'd describe them, if asked.

Mina, on the other hand, had none of the polish of her sisters. She was a natural beauty who didn't seem to care about manicures or salon appointments. Until this moment, he hadn't realized how much he admired that about her.

Meghan told him she was a professor at a North Carolina college. The other two sisters, Lauren and Desiree, were an architect and a psychotherapist, respectively. Lauren was noticeably pregnant. He'd guess about six months or more.

"You're just in time for lunch," Virginia announced after the introductions had been made. "Mina, your grandfather's fishermen friends supplied him with some fresh trout. I know you love that."

Virginia boldly took Jake's arm and led him inside.

As they went into the cabin, Mina brought up the rear. She wanted a private word with her grandfather who, she'd noticed, had been avoiding eye contact with her. When he did that, she knew he had something to feel guilty about.

She cornered him on the porch after everyone else

had gone inside. "This is your doing, isn't it?" she said, eyes narrowed.

"You know I can't lie to your mother," he said, not denying he'd blabbed. "She could tell by the sound of my voice that something was wrong. So she stuck the knife in and twisted, and I spilled my guts."

Mina didn't care for the visual, but she got his meaning. She smiled at him and hugged him. "I know, I know, Mom missed her calling. She could have been in the gestapo if they'd been accepting little half-black, half-Cherokee women back then."

Benjamin chuckled as they turned and went inside. Glancing at her sideways, he said, "You look none the worse for wear. Are you all right?"

"I survived," said Mina, "and that's what counts. Now, let's see if I can get through a fish dinner with my family."

It was a Southern fish fry with fresh trout, hush puppies, coleslaw and grits. The granddaughters, except for Mina, refused to eat grits. Their grandfather called them spoiled princesses with no regard for tradition.

"This really hits the spot." Jake complimented the cooks, who turned out to be Virginia and Benjamin. "I haven't had grits and fish that good since my grandmother made them."

Virginia's brows arched with curiosity. "Where was this, dear?" she asked.

"Crystal River, Florida," Jake answered, wiping his hands and mouth on a napkin.

"Didn't we pass through there a few years ago on our way to Key West?" Virginia asked Alfonse.

The general wrinkled his brow, thinking. "Yes, it's about two hours from Tampa, isn't it?"

Jake nodded, pleased that they were familiar with his childhood hometown. "Yes, it is. These days it's mostly known as one of the best places to observe manatees. Tourists go there to watch them and swim with them."

"I thought it was illegal for people to annoy sea creatures in that manner," said Meghan. Even though she was young, Jake could really see the professor persona shining through. She was very formal and pronounced her words precisely, as though she were standing in front of a class.

"Not in Crystal River," said Jake. "My grandparents say tourism based on the practice has been a real boost to the local economy."

"It just seems wrong to exploit them that way," insisted Meghan.

"I'm sure they take precautions so that the manatees aren't harmed," Mina put in.

She changed the subject by smiling at Lauren and asking, "So, Lauren, how are you and Colton Junior doing? You're glowing, so that must be a good sign. No more morning sickness?"

Lauren smiled slowly. "No, thank the Lord. Now all I have to contend with is a ravenous appetite. I've gained thirty pounds already, and that was supposed to be the maximum I could gain."

"It's that man she married," Virginia said disapprovingly. "He's turned into Super Chef. He cooks for her all the time, spoils her rotten. We're going to have to roll her into the delivery room."

Lauren laughed at her mother's comment. She and her mother used to butt heads on a regular basis, but shortly before Lauren's wedding, they had come to an understanding, and now their relationship was on solid ground. "Mother, I'm not that fat yet. And Colton is doing what any husband who loves his wife would do—he's taking very good care of me." She gave Mina a significant look that told Mina that Colton was taking care of her in more ways than cooking for her.

Mina found herself blushing, remembering how Jake had taken care of her not too long ago.

"That's wonderful," Mina said after clearing her throat and banishing the lusty thoughts from her head. She looked at Desiree. "And you, Desi. Is Colton's cousin, Decker, still stalking you?"

Desiree laughed. "Don't get me started on the subject of Decker Riley. I'm thinking of taking out a restraining order on him."

Lauren shook her head. "Do you hear her? She's *thinking* about it. Tell the truth, Desi. Some part of you is flattered by his attention."

"He *is* a successful attorney," Meghan said.

"And he has Riley genes, so he's a handsome devil," Lauren added.

"Too bad he's a nut," Desiree said, effectively putting an end to the conversation.

Desiree turned to Mina. "Mina, you've been up here more than a year now. How's *your* love life?"

Mina blushed furiously. She refused to even look at Jake for fear that someone in her family, a notoriously perceptive bunch, would realize the two of them were attracted to each other.

"Cut this nonsense out," Benjamin interrupted, inadvertently coming to Mina's rescue. "What I want to know is, did you get the bad guys?" He directed this query to Jake.

"We're making progress, Mr. Gaines. I'm afraid I'm not at liberty to discuss the case, but suffice it to say that some bad guys were taken down thanks to your granddaughter's bravery. She's the real heroine here," Jake answered.

The smile he bestowed on Mina was filled with admiration. Mina basked in the sunshine of his praise, and that, she knew, was her undoing because her mother's keen eyes hadn't missed a thing.

Fortunately for Mina, her mother hadn't been around when she was in a relationship with Keith. That courtship had taken place far away from North Carolina, and Mina had never brought Keith with her when she came home on leave. So Virginia had nothing with which to compare Mina's reaction to Jake. Mina was aware, however, that her mother knew her well. Mina had always been a self-contained child. She was a self-starter and self-motivator. She seemed to have been born with ambition. She excelled at everything: school, sports and especially her military training. Her mother had had no doubt that her second born would become a general someday.

Then Keith was killed, and Mina surprised them all by leaving the army. Mina knew some part of her mother was happy about that. No mother wanted her daughter in the midst of war. But Mina also knew that her mother was worried that she was cutting herself off, burying her emotions, hiding her head in the sand.

Today, Mina hoped her mom had seen that old spark back in her eyes and that she was happy for her.

That night, Mina lay in her bed in a darkened bedroom listening to the sounds of her sisters' breathing. Benjamin had given Virginia and Alfonse his bedroom, and he was bunking on the couch for the night. Mina's sisters had brought sleeping bags, save for Lauren, whose condition exempted her from having to sleep on the floor. She was sleeping in the bed with Mina.

Mina couldn't sleep. Her mind kept taking her back to this afternoon when she'd seen Jake off. After he'd gotten his few belongings from the cabin he'd stayed in, she walked him to his car and they'd said their goodbyes. She'd been too self-conscious to kiss him goodbye, knowing that her family was more than likely watching them, so they had stood there gazing longingly into each other's eyes.

"I'll call you when I get to Atlanta," Jake promised.

Mina wanted to reach up and caress his cheek, to feel the warmth of his skin one last time. She didn't know how long it would be before she got another chance to touch him.

Jake had told her a little more about the case a few hours ago after he'd gotten her alone. Charlie Betts had done a number on Danny. There had been no evidence in Charlie's residence that would lead the DEA to believe he was a drug kingpin. However, there had been copious evidence at Danny's more humble abode. Plus, a team of lawyers had shown up to represent Mario. They hadn't named Mario's benefactor, but it appeared that Charlie was supporting Mario, and that meant there was no way Mario was going to testify against him. Of course, Jake had told her, he hadn't believed for a second that Mario was going to testify anyway.

"Be careful," she said, when what she really wanted to say was, *I'll miss you.*

"I want you to be careful, too," Jake said with a smile. His golden eyes devoured her face and his gaze lingered on her mouth. "I really want to kiss you," he whispered. "But I know that would be inappropriate. So I'll shake your hand."

It was the most sensual handshake Mina had ever experienced. Desire shot through her, electrifying her. Their eyes met.

"It's been a pleasure," she said, her voice husky.

"A real pleasure," Jake agreed. The timbre of his voice was so sexy, it made Mina tremble inside.

She sighed. "Go, before I do something stupid like kiss you anyway."

She stepped aside so he could climb into the SUV.

Jake gave her a mock salute and said, "See you in my dreams, Captain," before he drove away.

Already regretting that she hadn't kissed him, Mina smiled as she watched him go.

Now, as she lay in bed, the kiss that hadn't happened was on her mind. Lauren shifted uncomfortably beside her. "I know why *I'm* awake," Lauren said. "I can't get comfortable with this boy moving all night long. What's your excuse?"

"Just restless, I guess," Mina said softly.

"You should have kissed him," Lauren said.

"Yeah, M," Meghan piped in. "I would have kissed the hell out of him."

"Me, too," Desiree said.

Mina laughed. "So you *were* watching us!"

"And taking bets," Lauren told her, pulling herself up in bed, her enormous belly sticking out like an overripe watermelon.

Mina reached over and switched on the bedside lamp, sure that this was the beginning of one of their all-night gossip sessions.

"I won twenty bucks," Meghan told Mina. "Honey, there was so much sexual tension between you and Jake that we couldn't contain our happiness for you. But sorry, sis, you were entirely too keyed up to go for that goodbye kiss."

"I lost," Desiree said, climbing out of her sleeping bag and sitting cross-legged on it. "I was rooting for you."

Meghan did the same, and then the three sisters turned and looked expectantly at Mina.

"Go ahead, tell us," Lauren coaxed. "Is Mr. DEA a good lover?"

Mina laughed. "I'm not going to discuss my sex life…."

"Her sex life," Meghan interrupted. "She admits she has one!"

"Well, he looks like he's in great physical condition," said Desiree. "He must have a lot of stamina."

Mina flushed and made the mistake of fanning her face in front of her sisters.

"Oh, my, is he that enthusiastic a lover?" Lauren asked, her eyes alight with humor. "Good for you, girl!"

"I didn't say a word," Mina protested.

"You didn't have to," Desiree, the psychotherapist, observed. "Your body language says it all."

"You're having fun," Meghan said, smiling widely. "It's about time."

Chapter 10

Even though Jake's cover was blown, he was still on the Charlie Betts case, and the following week he went to two funerals in the line of duty.

The first was John Monahan's. Jake had been the one to break the news of John's death to his widow, Lynn. She was already aware that John was trying to give up his life of crime and had been hopeful he'd succeed. Jake had been happy to confirm John's intentions and at least give her something to feel proud about. So, on this rainy day, when he showed up at the graveside memorial, Lynn had given him a wan smile and a nod of acknowledgment.

Jake was also there to observe. He had not expected Charlie Betts to put in an appearance, but the short, stocky, impeccably dressed criminal had walked up with two bodyguards in tow, one holding an umbrella over him while the other brought up the rear. When Charlie first spotted Jake he frowned and narrowed his eyes at him, a sneer twisting his thin lips. But then his facial features relaxed, and he smiled at him and mouthed, "Asshole."

Jake kept his expression neutral. He didn't want to antagonize Betts at John's funeral and end up in a brawl. It was disrespectful, and Lynn had gone through enough.

Charlie chose to keep things low-key, as well, during the service. However, later, as Jake was walking to his car, Betts and his bodyguards waylaid him.

Jake turned and faced them. "It was so nice of you to come and pay your respects to the man you killed."

Charlie had dirty-blond hair like his younger brother, Danny, but his was cut by an expensive stylist. Everything about him said money, but to Jake, no amount of money could wipe away the stench of corruption.

Charlie sighed as though he were tired. "*You* can talk. You killed my brother."

"No, Charlie," Jake disagreed, "*you* killed your brother. When you brought him into your business, you signed his death warrant. He gave me a message to deliver to you. He said, 'Tell Charlie I died like a man.'"

For a second, Jake thought he saw a modicum of regret in Charlie Betts's gaze when he heard his brother's last words. Then those cold blue eyes got even colder, and Betts said through clenched teeth, "You'll pay for killing my brother."

"I'm already paying," Jake told him. "Every day I have to live with the fact that Danny used me to commit suicide. You see, he couldn't face prison, and he definitely couldn't face you. Now, you live with *that,* Charlie."

Charlie leaned toward Jake, and following his cue, his bodyguards put their hands on their concealed weapons. They were waiting for the go-ahead from Charlie. Jake briefly wondered if they were bold enough to shoot him down in a cemetery filled with mourners.

But Charlie gestured for his bodyguards to stand down. The men relaxed and returned to their power stances on either side of him.

Jake didn't relax, though. He was ready to defend himself, if that's what it came to. But his safety wasn't foremost in his mind. More than two hundred innocent bystanders' lives would have been in jeopardy if Betts had given his men the signal to act.

"Not here," said Charlie. "I'll be seeing you when you least expect it, Jake." With that, he walked off.

Jake didn't allow himself to relax until Betts's car was exiting through the gates of the cemetery.

The second funeral took place the next day. This time, Jake didn't show his face. Instead, he watched the graveside memorial service from his car. Danny's service was not as well attended as John Monahan's. From surveillance photos, Jake recognized Danny's mother, Sharon, a woman in her sixties who still worked as a waitress in an Atlanta diner. John had told him her story on a flight to Canada. It seemed Charlie and Danny's mother disapproved of her sons' method of making money. She wouldn't have anything to do with them. But, apparently, she'd set aside her feelings to be here to see her youngest son put into the ground.

She wasn't happy about it, though. Jake watched as she walked up to Charlie and started gesticulating wildly. Jake couldn't hear a word that was being said, but she had Charlie backing away from her. She ended her tirade by slapping him hard across the face, and then she turned and walked away.

Jake took out his binoculars and watched Charlie Betts's reddened face. A single tear rolled down his cheek. Whatever his mother said had gotten to him. Or maybe she just had a good right arm.

It was the last week of September, and Mina was staying busy around the lodge. Today, Saturday, she was leading a hike to Mingo Falls, which was on the Eastern Cherokee Indian Reservation. Six lodge guests followed her through the forest, over some steep trails that culminated at the 120-foot falls, one of the most remarkable in the southern Appalachians.

The trail leading to the falls could be difficult for some, so Mina frequently told the guests to tread carefully.

"The name Mingo," one of the guests, a redhead in her thirties, asked. "Is that a Cherokee word?"

"It is," said Mina, smiling at the woman. "It means big bear. The Cherokee venerate the bear."

"I noticed that depictions of bears are everywhere in the town of Cherokee," said the same woman.

"Like I said, the Cherokee people admire the bear. You'll hear it often mentioned in their stories, their ceremonies, and see it in their artwork."

"Do you know any more Cherokee words?" asked the woman.

"You'll hear the word *shi-yo* a lot," Mina told her. "It's a common greeting." She paused on the trail, cupped a hand to her ear and said, "Do you hear that?"

The guests all smiled when they heard the rushing waters of the falls. Mina motioned for them to continue walking. Soon, they were standing atop a ridge from which they had a spectacular view of Mingo Falls.

There were sharp intakes of breath as they took in the natural beauty of the sight. Mina smiled. Mingo Falls never failed to impress.

Later, when she was walking across the lawn to her cabin that night, she took out her cell phone and dialed Jake's number.

They had spoken on the phone every night since they'd parted, sharing information all new couples long to know about each other, such as birthdates, favorite books and movies.

He answered right away. "Hello, beautiful, what does your sky look like tonight?"

Mina peered overhead. "A blanket of sooty blackness, liberally sprinkled with stars," she said, a bit breathlessly.

"I wish I were there," Jake said.

"Not as much as I do," Mina told him. Then she said, "Happy birthday. Did you do anything special today?"

"This is the most special thing I've done today," he told her, his voice filled with longing.

Mina smiled. "That's sweet. What did you think of my card?"

Jake laughed softly. "It was the talk of the office."

Mina's face flushed with embarrassment. She had written some personal things that had been meant only for his eyes.

"I was reading it for probably the tenth time when one of my coworkers looked over my shoulder and read it. Now they're calling me MM."

"MM?" Mina asked curiously.

"Mina's man," Jake explained with a chuckle. "I'll never live it down."

"It has a nice ring to it," Mina said, laughing softly.

"Yes, it does," Jake agreed, his voice growing husky with longing. Mina could hear the sound of an elevator's arrival on his end.

"You're at the elevator," she commented.

"I went to get some takeout for dinner," Jake said. "I'm heading back up now."

"It's kind of late for dinner," Mina said. It was nearly ten o'clock at night.

"I had a long day," said Jake tiredly. "I was at the hospital with my brother for most of it."

"Something happened to Leo?"

"A couple of guys jumped him when he was jogging in the park earlier today. He can handle himself most of the time, but there were two of them. He gave as good as he got. But he still ended up badly bruised."

"But he's going to be okay?"

"Yes, he'll be fine."

"Did the police catch the guys who jumped him?"

"Yes, they caught them," said Jake. Mina thought she heard some hesitation in his voice.

"Jake?"

"They work for Charlie Betts."

Mina's mind was racing, calculating, reasoning out what he'd said and *not* said. "You think he's going after your loved ones, don't you?"

"I wouldn't put it past him. He said he would make me pay for killing Danny."

"He's losing it," Mina said. "This is no way to keep a low profile. Do you think he's about to slip up? The way you described his past behavior, he was always too smart to try something like this. He hasn't got Danny around to blame, now."

"Yeah, he's coming apart at the seams," Jake agreed. He went on to tell her about the scene between Charlie and his mother, Sharon, at the graveside service for Danny.

When he'd finished, he said, "I won't be coming back up there until he's behind bars, Mina. Or dead, whichever comes first."

Mina knew he was saying she was on Betts's radar.

But she wanted to see him so badly, she felt compelled to argue the point anyway. "How could he know about us? Mario knows where I live, but why would Mario point a finger at me? He didn't know you and I were more than DEA agent and kidnap victim."

"No, but I think I'm being followed. I don't want to lead them to you."

Mina felt deflated. "Oh, I see."

"And I want you to arm yourself," Jake said. "You do have a weapon?"

"I'm proficient with several weapons, yes, but I haven't been to a firing range since I left the army. I lost interest."

"But you do own a gun?"

"Yes, I have both a pistol and a rifle," she answered resignedly.

"Well, get them out and clean them, and go to the range and get in a little practice," Jake said. "Mina, I don't want to spook you, but I don't want anything to happen to you, either. I know we haven't known each other for very long, but you mean a lot to me. I can hear the reluctance to arm yourself in your voice. Do this for me, please."

His tone was what made her agree to do as he asked. He was deadly serious. "I will," she promised.

He gave a sigh of relief. "Thank you. Now, what else has been going on? Has your sister had her baby yet?"

"No, she has three more months to go," Mina said, laughing as she sat down on the edge of the cabin's porch. "She just *looks* like she's about to give birth."

"What do I know?" Jake said, also laughing. "I've never had the pleasure of becoming a father."

"You sound like you've given it some thought, though," Mina observed.

"Of course I have. I'm going to need sons to help run the farm," Jake joked.

"Are we back to that fantasy again?" Mina joked right along with him.

"Four sons and maybe a daughter, or two."

"And a very strong wife. Six children? She's going to need her strength."

"We would make beautiful children together," Jake mused.

Mina laughed really hard then. "Let's go on another date before we start talking about having children."

"Deal," said Jake. "I'll wait until our six-month anniversary before picking out baby names."

"You're such a romantic!"

"All jokes aside, I can't get you off my mind. I really miss you, Mina."

"That's so sweet." Mina sighed. "I miss you, too."

Jake chuckled softly. "I'd better go before I embarrass myself further. Good night."

"Good night," Mina said, her voice husky.

After she'd hung up the phone, she sighed wistfully and gazed up at the star-filled sky. "Oh, boy, I think I'm falling for that sweet-talker."

Jake was obliged to write up what had happened on the plane just before it crashed in order to complete the file on John Monahan. He'd been avoiding it, but the next day, after talking to Mina, which always buoyed his spirits, he tackled the task.

When he got to the part where John said he hadn't anticipated that Charlie Betts would have his home phone tapped, it got him thinking: Had anyone followed up and searched the Monahan home for bugs?

He got up from his desk and walked across the huge office to Hoyt Granger's office. He knocked and heard Granger's gravelly voice say, "Come in!"

Jake opened the door and stuck his head in. "I'd like to send a team to the Monahan house to check for listening devices."

"What's your reason for doing this?" Granger asked.

Jake told him and then said, "If there are none, then we know there must be a leak somewhere."

"Are you saying someone here is on Betts's payroll?"

"I'm saying I want to eliminate the possibility," Jake said. "Somehow, Betts found out about me and took the opportunity to get rid of me and Monahan. If he didn't bug the Monahans' home, then someone provided him with the information."

Frowning, Granger said with obvious reluctance, "All right, do it. But keep it quiet. I don't want paranoia to set in around here."

Jake nodded and left. Of course he would keep it quiet. He certainly didn't want to tip off any mole that someone was looking for him or her.

He glanced at his watch as he returned to his desk.

It was a quarter past noon. He wondered if Lynn Monahan was home. If he could get her permission to search the house, he wouldn't need a court order.

He didn't need a team to go in and check for bugs. He could do it himself. That plan would work better. There would be fewer people trampling Lynn Monahan's nice floors, and she was already comfortable with him.

He made a quick call, and Lynn told him to come on over. The kids were in school; she wasn't doing anything except cleaning and welcomed a break from that. She sounded casual, but Jake was sure he'd heard a nervous note in her voice. She undoubtedly would rest better if she was certain there were no listening devices in her home.

Lynn, a petite African-American woman in her late twenties, with long, dark brown, wavy hair that she wore down her back, greeted him at the door with a smile. "Special Agent Wolfe," she said pleasantly.

Jake smiled back. "Mrs. Monahan. Thanks for allowing me to come over on such short notice."

"You got my curiosity up," Lynn admitted. She gestured for him to come inside.

Jake stepped into the foyer of the two-story house. The first thing he noticed was a lovely photograph of the interracial couple and their two small children on the hall table. They were a happy-looking bunch.

Lynn noticed him looking at the photo and smiled. "We had that taken less than a year ago. I never thought that only a few months later, John wouldn't be here." Tears glinted in her eyes.

Jake said, "I'm so sorry. I want you to know that we're doing everything in our power to make the person responsible for John's death pay for his crimes."

Lynn wiped her tears away with the back of her hand. She looked up at him. "Don't take this the wrong way, but why do you care? John was a criminal, too."

Jake smiled slowly. "Yes, but he was trying to do the right thing when he died. He told me he wanted to become the type of husband and father you could be proud of."

Lynn's eyes filled with tears again. "He said that?" she asked, astonished.

"He loved you very much," Jake told her.

Lynn blew air between her lips and took a deep breath, pulling herself together. Standing straighter, she said, "You have the run of the house, Special Agent Wolfe. If there are any bugs in here, please remove them and take them with you!"

"In my rush to get over here, I forgot I might need a ladder to check light fixtures," Jake said. "Do you have one?"

"In the garage," Lynn said. "Just go through the kitchen to the garage, and you'll see it leaning against the wall."

Jake thanked her and went to get the ladder. Lynn left him to his own devices, going off to another part of the house.

An hour later, he had scoured the house from the landline phones to every lamp and light fixture, but had found no listening devices. He even checked all of the heating and air conditioning vents.

He returned the ladder to the same spot where he'd gotten it. Then he called to Lynn. "Mrs. Monahan!"

Lynn returned to the living room from the laundry room, carrying a bundle of folded linen. She looked at him curiously. "Any luck?"

Jake smiled. "You're officially bug free," he told her.

She sighed. "That's a load off. Thank you. I'm relieved to hear that a conversation between me and John didn't lead to his death."

It hadn't occurred to Jake that she might be experiencing feelings of guilt. He nodded solemnly. He really didn't know what to say to that. "If you should need anything, don't hesitate to call me," he said as he went into his coat pocket and retrieved one of his cards.

Lynn accepted it and said, "Thank you. I hope you all find some way to catch Charlie Betts. He's a slippery snake."

"That he is," agreed Jake.

She saw him to the door, and Jake made his exit.

As he jogged down the front steps, he wondered who the mole could be. He'd worked out of the Atlanta office for six years now. He felt close to the agents and support staff, as if he could trust them with his life. Obviously one of them had found Charlie Betts's money more enticing than staying loyal to the team. But then, money had always been a potent temptation.

If he were going with his gut, there was no one

whose recent behavior sent up any red flags. But the evidence was clear. The Monahan house was not bugged; therefore, someone was providing Betts with information.

He would have to find a way to flush him or her out.

Chapter 11

Mina was listening to an Edward Sharpe and the Magnetic Zeros song on her iPod as she jogged. She loved the group's cross-genre music. It was mid-October, and she hadn't seen Jake in a month, although they spoke daily.

She jogged past one of the guests on the trail. He was a mild-mannered guy in his early forties who seemed to always be off walking somewhere. A solitary guy, he hadn't signed up for any of the lodge's activities yet. But Mina supposed some of the guests came here for the quiet and not for the group activities.

"Good morning, Mr. Weinstein," Mina called to him as she jogged by. "Hope you have a lovely day!"

"You too, Ms. Gaines." He returned the greeting.

Mina couldn't place his accent, but he was very pale, as though he didn't spend much time in the sun, so she thought he might be one of the many northerners who stayed with them. He wore glasses, and his brown hair, thinning on top, was short and unruly. It had a tendency to stick out on the sides, which made him look harried and unkempt.

Mina ran on. She was hoping to get in five miles before lunchtime. This was one of those rare days when she didn't have a group to take on a trail ride or a hike. In fact, she had the day pretty much to herself. She wished Jake were here to spend it with her. But Jake was busy trying to track down Charlie Betts, who had disappeared from the Atlanta area. The agency didn't know how he'd done it. They had him under constant surveillance, yet one day he was there, and the next he was gone.

Jake told her he suspected that Charlie had employed a body double, someone his size, skin and hair color, someone who could easily pass for him from a distance. While the agents watching him were distracted by the double, Charlie could have walked past the agents wearing a clever disguise.

Mina was weary of all the subterfuge. She wished Charlie Betts had never existed. His presence in the world was keeping her from Jake, the man she could easily fall for if given a bit more time with him. But all she had were her memories of the innocent night they'd shared in Asheville. Wonderful memories, for sure, but memories weren't enough.

She almost regretted letting her guard down with

Jake. Her loneliness had been more bearable than this constant ache to be with him again. You couldn't miss what you never had. And now that she had Jake Wolfe in her life, she craved him like crazy.

Two days later, Jake was having a sandwich at his desk when the phone on it rang. He answered it with, "Special Agent Jake Wolfe."

The call was from the county jail. Mario Fuentes was using some of his meager phone privileges to call him. Jake knew whatever Fuentes had to say must be important.

"Mario," Jake said. "How're they treating you?"

"Listen, man, I ain't got time for chitchat," Mario said urgently. "This has been bothering me since it happened four days ago, and I gotta get it off my chest."

"Go ahead," Jake said.

"Charlie came to see me," Mario told him, "and the only thing he wanted to talk about was Miss Mina."

Jake's heart thudded with anxiety when Charlie Betts's and Mina's names were mentioned in the same sentence. This couldn't be good.

"What did you tell him?"

"Not a damned thing," Mario said, sounding defiant. "I like Miss Mina. She's got guts, you know?"

"I thought you were trying to get back in his good graces since he sent a team of lawyers to defend you," Jake put in.

"He didn't send those lawyers to defend me," Mario said. "He sent them to warn me to keep my mouth shut. I ain't no fool. Like I told you, I'm doomed and I know it. But anyway, would you stop interrupting me? I'm tryin' to tell you something important."

"Sorry, I'm listening," Jake said encouragingly.

"Charlie's changed," Mario said. "He's not the cold, calculating bastard he used to be. Okay, well, he still is that bastard, but he's gone loco now, too, man. I could see it in his eyes. He kept rambling on about Danny and how he never thought he'd get killed. He wouldn't have sent him if he'd known he'd get killed. Then he started saying his momma never loved him. Danny was her favorite. And he'd gotten Danny killed, so his momma told him she wished it was him that was dead instead of Danny. She said he ruined Danny's life. But the scariest thing he said was, 'I need a vacation. I've always liked the mountains.' That chilled me to the bone."

It chilled Jake to the bone, too. "He's going after Mina," Jake said, more to himself than to Mario.

"That's my guess," Mario said. "You've gotta do something!"

"Thanks, Mario," Jake said hurriedly. "I mean, really, thank you." He hung up.

He got to his feet and grabbed his suit jacket. He was tugging it on as he headed for the elevator. His hand went to the shoulder holster with his weapon in it, just to make sure it was there.

His mind was moving at a fast clip. Granger wasn't in the office, so there was no need, and definitely no time, to track him down and fill him in on the situation. Jake weighed travel options. If he drove, it would take him three hours to reach Cherokee. However, by helicopter it would take much less time.

In his rush, he collided with Neil Olsen, one of the agents he worked with. Neil, a much slighter guy, was knocked off his feet. Jake reached down and helped him up. "Sorry, man, I didn't see you."

Neil eyed him with concern. "Anything I can help you with, buddy?"

"Just need to be somewhere, like, yesterday," Jake told him.

"Is somebody in trouble?" Neil asked. "Don't go running off half-cocked. If you need backup, just say the word."

Jake paused. That might be a good idea, to have backup. There was no telling what he'd be walking into. Betts might not be alone. Plus, Neil was a helicopter pilot. A definite advantage when he was thinking of taking one of the agency's helicopters without permission.

Jake gave Neil a quick rundown of the situation. Both men agreed that the fastest way to get to Cherokee would be via helicopter.

When they got to the building's helipad, two choppers were sitting there. Jake looked at Neil. "There's no time to requisition one of these babies. Are you up for some grand theft this afternoon?"

"I'm with you," said Neil with a grin. He was a Southern boy, born and bred, who was used to driving muscle cars, getting his pickup truck stuck in the mud on weekends and blaring country music while he was doing it. He lived for excitement, which was one reason he'd become a DEA agent. "Let's fire this thing up," he cried as he got into the pilot's seat of one helicopter, which was black with the DEA emblem on the side.

In a matter of minutes, Jake was buckled up beside him, and Neil had run through the list of items he had to check on the helicopter before starting the rotors. They both wore dark glasses and headsets. Neil piloted them up and away from downtown Atlanta.

"Make sure you check the fuel gauge," Jake joked. "I've had a little trouble with those lately."

Neil laughed shortly. "Don't worry. We have enough fuel to get us there and back."

"I just hope we're not too late." Jake was worried. He fell silent as the helicopter left the city of Atlanta behind and headed north.

Mina was on a trail ride with the nice, but seriously introverted, Mr. Weinstein when her cell phone vibrated. Frankly, she was surprised to feel it, because she'd thought they were out of range. But obviously they weren't high enough in the mountains yet, since she still had a signal. She reached into her jacket pocket and got the phone. She saw immediately that it was Jake calling.

"Excuse me, Mr. Weinstein," she said. "I need to take this."

Cinnamon came to a stop with a bit of prodding from Mina, and Mina pressed talk. "Hi, handsome, what's up?"

On his end, Jake breathed a sigh of relief. "Mina, are you all right?"

"Of course, I'm on a trail ride right now. We're a couple miles from the lodge, but I'm just fine. Why do you ask?"

He quickly told her what he suspected. Then he described Charlie Betts for her. "His appearance could be a bit different now, though. He might have dyed his hair, put in contacts, that kind of thing."

"No," Mina told him. "I haven't seen anyone who fits that description."

"Have you had any new guests arrive in the past four days?"

"Yes, several," Mina said. "A couple from Boston, two male friends from San Francisco…" She didn't finish because the only other person to check in recently was right behind her. And if she weren't mistaken, the sound she'd just heard was the sound of Mr. Weinstein pulling back the slide to load the chamber of an automatic weapon.

She turned around and looked at Mr. Weinstein. He was smiling and holding a Walther P-series pistol in his right hand. He silently motioned for her to hang up the phone.

Mina started to say something else, but he shook his head. She thought it wise to put the phone away.

Only a few miles from Cherokee, Jake uttered an expletive and put his phone back in his jacket pocket. They were already over the Great Smoky Mountains, and Neil was taking the helicopter down so they could scan the forest.

"She stopped talking in the middle of her sentence," Jake said. "He must be on the trail ride with her, but I have no idea if anyone else is out there with them. Not that they'd stand in Betts's way."

"Did she mention anything that would help us pinpoint their location?"

"She said they were about two miles from the lodge," Jake said.

Mina smiled as she regarded Charlie Betts. It was funny. Somehow, she'd envisioned him bigger than he was. He was perhaps three inches taller than her five-five frame, and he was carrying excess weight that manifested itself mostly in a soft midsection and a double chin.

His benign appearance didn't make him any less terrifying, though, especially with that pistol pointing at her head. "Hello, Mr. Betts," she said. "You really had me fooled."

He smiled at her, seemingly pleased she'd fallen for his performance. "I've enjoyed observing you, Mina. You're a beautiful woman, and very personable, too. I can see why Jake loves you."

"You've got the wrong girl," Mina told him, much more cheerily than she felt at the moment. "Jake and I just met. He doesn't love me."

"The way I hear he was bowled over by that birthday card you sent him says otherwise," Charlie commented dryly.

Mina's eyes stretched wide at the mention of the card, but she didn't say anything. His eyes gleamed with satisfaction. He seemed to be pleased he'd shocked her with his knowledge of Jake's life.

Midnight, the horse Betts was riding, began prancing in place. Mina knew how skittish the horse could be around loud noises and hoped nothing happened to disrupt the silence of the woods around them. It would be a shame if Betts's gun went off accidentally and she got shot before she could come up with a way out of this predicament.

"If you shoot me, Midnight will throw you," she cautioned him. "Remember, as part of your instructions before we left the barn, I told you how nervous she gets around loud noises."

"I'm not going to shoot you," he told her calmly. "I've got a better idea." Continuing to hold the gun on her, he ordered, "Get off the horse."

Mina complied and tossed the reins over Cinnamon's powerful neck. She hit Cinnamon on the rump, and the horse took off at a trot toward home. Then she looked up at him. "Are we walking from here?"

"You are," he told her. "You see, for the past three days I've been taking long walks, thinking. My brother died out here, and I think it's only fitting that you do, as well. But I'm not a martyr. After the deed I'll need an escape route, so I've arranged to be met at a certain spot in the woods about three miles from your lodge. We're almost there now. My ride might already be waiting for me." He impatiently gestured for her to head south.

"So that's why you suddenly had an urge to go on a trail ride today," Mina said as she turned and began walking.

He smirked. "I thought you'd be happy to do it since poor shy-guy me hadn't been doing much of anything exciting while I've been here."

"And you're right," Mina said. "I thought you were finally beginning to get in the swing of things and actually enjoying yourself for once."

"Oh, I *am*," Betts said. His green eyes sparkled with delight.

Mina looked intently at his smug face. When Jake had described him, he'd said Betts had cold blue eyes. She remembered that Danny's eyes were green. "You're wearing green contacts in honor of Danny," she said, and from the startled expression on his face she knew she'd touched a nerve.

"What do you know about Danny?" he rasped, his pale face turning red.

"Haven't you heard?" Mina said. "He and two other men broke into our house, roughed up my grandfather and threatened us unless we took them to the plane, which I wound up doing. Oh, I think I know a lot about your brother."

"You don't know anything! Keep moving," he yelled. Midnight whinnied and began prancing in place again.

"And you don't know jack about horses," Mina countered. She smiled at him. "How much farther do we have to go? Maybe you can regale me with stories of your conquests as a drug dealer. I've always wondered if movies like *Scarface* are close to reality. Have you ever gunned anybody down while yelling, 'Say hello to my little friend'?"

Charlie laughed. "You're very funny, Mina. But soon, you won't be laughing, you'll be dying."

"I'm pretty sure no matter what I say, it isn't going to change your mind," said Mina. "So I'd just as well say what I want to say."

"You know, I like you," Charlie told her as he rode Midnight. "But I'm still going to kill you. And enjoy it."

"I have no doubt you will," Mina said unhappily. Then she fell silent and simply walked in the direction he indicated with his gun.

After about ten minutes of silence, Charlie asked, "Were you there when Wolfe killed Danny?"

"No, when we reached the plane Danny and the two other men left me some distance away while they went to check out the plane. I was hiding in the woods when Jake had to shoot Danny."

"So you didn't see what happened," Charlie reiterated.

"No."

"But you believed Wolfe when he said it was in self-defense?"

"Yes, I believed him."

"Why?"

"Because he's a good man, and he wouldn't kill anyone in cold blood."

"Just because he's a DEA agent doesn't make him a

good man," Charlie said. "He infiltrated my organization. What makes you think I couldn't infiltrate his?"

Even though her life was in jeopardy, the mystery
lover in Mina raised its head at that moment. "Fascinating," she said. "You have a DEA agent in your
pocket?"

"I'm beginning to think you're enjoying this,
Mina. You sound almost impressed." Charlie smiled
slowly. "I like a woman who can roll with anything.
Too bad I'm going to have to kill you to avenge my
brother."

"Damn," said Neil, as loud beeps and a cacophony
of other noises assaulted their ears. Red lights on the
control panel signified mechanical problems. Luckily, Neil saw a clearing below that was large enough
to safely set down the helicopter. "I'll have to take
her down," he said resignedly.

Déjà vu, Jake thought grimly. He tensed as Neil
landed none too gently. Neil cut the motor, and they
got out of the helicopter. Jake looked at Neil. "Do you
think you can fix it, or are we footing it from here?"

Neil didn't answer but climbed into the back of
the helicopter as though he was looking for a tool
box or something. When he came out he was holding a gun on Jake.

Jake didn't register surprise. "I figured you didn't
just run into me when I was leaving. You've been
keeping an eye on me for Betts."

Neil walked around the helicopter, gun trained on
Jake. They stood a few feet apart in front of the ma-

chine, Neil shaking his head sadly. "I'm sorry it has to come to this, Jake, truly I am. But blood is thicker than water."

"You're related to Betts?" Jake asked incredulously.

"First cousins," Neil confirmed proudly. "Both of us Georgia boys. Born to and raised by sisters."

"How long have you been on his payroll—from the beginning, or did you sign on recently?"

"From the beginning," Neil answered. "How do you think he's always been one step ahead of us?"

"Then why did it take you so long to tell him about me?" Jake wanted to know.

"A negotiation for more money," Neil said. "Charlie's always been a cheap bastard. I told him I had some key information, but he didn't want to pay me what it was worth."

"How much *was* it worth?" Jake asked. His attention was on Neil's eyes and not on his trigger finger. The eyes were the first indicators of when a person was getting ready to shoot. Most people flinched and blinked just before they pulled the trigger, either out of distaste for what was about to happen, or to instinctively protect their eyes.

"A cool million," Neil told him. "I plan to retire shortly after you meet your maker, Jake."

"That's not enough money to retire on," Jake scoffed.

"Oh, I've been squirreling money away for a long time now," Neil informed him. Jake wondered why men like Neil got chatty when they thought they had the upper hand. No need to lie at this point in the game? His victim was going to be dead soon, anyway. Why not tell him the whole truth?

Biding his time, Jake continued talking. "How're you going to explain my death? Surely you're not going to use your own gun."

"I'm not going to kill you, Jake," Neil told him. He gestured for Jake to look behind him. Jake turned and saw Mina walking out of the woods, with Charlie Betts following her on a horse. When Mina had gotten a few yards in front of him, Betts dismounted and yelled, "The gang's all here. Let's get this party started."

That's when Midnight reared up on her hind legs and kicked him clear into a nearby clump of bramble bushes.

Mina watched the scene with eyes stretched in horror and, she had to admit, a little admiration for Midnight. Apparently the horse had had enough of that horse's ass who'd been riding her all afternoon.

It was clear from the lack of any kind of moaning, and in fact any sound at all, that Betts had been knocked unconscious.

But Mina had also seen what was unfolding in front of the helicopter: Jake was being held at gunpoint. She saw the surprised expression on the face of the guy with the gun when Midnight kicked Betts into the bushes, and she saw Jake hit the ground and roll, reach for his weapon in its shoulder holster and come back up onto one knee in a firing stance. The guy with the gun went to pull the trigger but was too slow. Jake shot him in the shoulder and he lost his grip on his weapon. It fell to the ground, and he followed suit a second later and began howling with pain. Mina hadn't even needed to pull the weapon that she'd been wearing under her jacket in a neat little shoulder holster ever since Jake had told her she needed to arm herself.

She'd been waiting for the opportunity to use it on Charlie Betts, but Midnight had taken care of Betts for her.

She went and calmed down Midnight, speaking soothingly to her. The big horse was soon standing serenely while Mina fed her an apple she'd gotten from her saddlebags.

Mina saw Jake walk to the man he'd shot and help him to his feet. He pulled off the guy's jacket, rolled it into a ball and made him press it against the shoulder wound to stanch the bleeding. Then he handcuffed him to the helicopter and proceeded to pat him down, obviously checking to see if he had any more weapons on him. Satisfied he didn't, Jake turned and began walking toward her with a big smile on his face.

Finally, Mina heard a moan from the bushes and went to look down at Charlie Betts. He looked understandably woozy about the eyes. He tried to sit up, but couldn't and lay back down. His gun was lying several feet away. Mina picked it up and put the safety on. She looked up, saw Jake running toward her and carefully dropped the gun on the ground at her feet.

By that time, Jake was picking her up in his arms, hugging her tightly and kissing her breathless.

"Thank God you're safe in my arms again," he said, holding her close. "I don't know what I would've done if anything had happened to you. I'm so sorry that, because of me, Betts came after you." He held her at arm's length, searching her face. "You *are* all right, aren't you?"

"I'm perfectly fine," Mina assured him with a smile. She was so happy to see him, she figured that smile would be glued to her face for the foreseeable future.

Jake hugged her again. "Well, it's over now. Betts, if he lives, is going to prison for a long time."

Mina glanced over her shoulder at the man handcuffed to the helicopter. "And who's that?"

Jake narrowed his eyes at Neil, who was leaning weakly against the helicopter. "He's DEA, too. He was Betts's inside man for years. I'd better call someone so that he can get to a hospital."

A pitiful moan came from the direction of the bramble bushes.

"The notorious Charlie Betts is alive," said Mina.

Jake looked at Mina. "Do you think you can fly us out of here?"

Mina smiled slowly as her gaze fell on the helicopter. "That's a CH-47 Chinook. Of course I can fly it."

A few minutes later, Jake and Mina had carried Betts on board the craft with the drug lord moaning in agony all the way. Jake was helping Neil into the helicopter when Neil muttered, "She's not authorized to fly this aircraft."

"If you like, we can just take Betts to a hospital and leave you here for someone else to pick up," said Jake irritably.

Neil shut up after that and behaved himself.

Hearing the exchange, Mina just smiled, and after making sure the throttle was fully open and the machine had achieved the proper rpm, she raised the collective and the craft lifted into the air. Soon both her hands and feet were working in tandem as she smoothly piloted the helicopter above the treetops.

Sitting beside her, Jake laughed. "Just like Beggar's Canyon back home, huh?"

Mina laughed too. "I haven't lost my touch."

Chapter 12

"Jake, are you nuts?" Mina giggled as Jake swept her up into his arms and carried her over the threshold of his apartment in Atlanta. Now she knew why he'd asked her to hold onto the bouquet of fresh flowers he'd bought her and the bottle of wine. It was so that he would have both hands free with which to carry out this maneuver.

"No, just glad to have you all to myself." He laughed and kicked the door closed.

Setting her down, he grinned at her. "Look, Mina, we've been through hell together, so now let's make tonight our personal paradise."

They had spent the last few hours answering questions, first at the hospital and then at DEA headquarters. Now was the time to kick back, relax and, Mina hoped, fulfill the sweet promise of all that pent-up sexual tension she had been feeling between them.

Mina set the flowers and the bottle of wine on the hall table and looked around her. Jake's living room was huge, with hardwood floors and contemporary furnishings in brown leather with modern accents. It was masculine, but very tasteful. "Nice place," she told him.

Jake smiled his pleasure. "I'm glad you like it." He glanced down at his clothes. The white dress shirt was dirty, his suit trousers had a rip in the right leg and he didn't know where his tie was.

"I'm a mess," he said.

Mina surveyed her own state. "I could use a shower myself."

Their eyes met and held, and slow smiles spread over their features. Then, the next instant, they were in each other's arms, kissing passionately while simultaneously undressing each other.

Mina broke off the kiss with, "Just so there are no interruptions this time—you *do* have condoms?"

Jake nodded affirmatively and resumed kissing her.

Good, thought Mina, *because I'm so ready.* But then, unbidden, images of her and Keith making love flashed through her mind, and she froze.

Jake immediately sensed the change in her and raised his head. He held her firmly by the shoulders as his eyes met hers. "Is something the matter?" he asked softly, his tone warm and concerned. "Because if we're moving too fast for you, I'm willing to wait...."

Mina was touched by his understanding, but she was beginning to wonder if she'd ever get over this stumbling block. Logically, she knew Keith would want her to move on. They had talked about this very situation. They'd both agreed that should anything happen to either of them they would want the other to find happiness with someone else. A soldier was usually clear-eyed about death. They knew that it could come for them at any time. And the world kept turning, with or without them.

Mina and Jake stood looking deeply into each other's eyes.

"Jake, it's not a question of time, I don't believe. It's a question of whether I'll ever get Keith out of my head every time you and I get close to making love."

Jake smiled knowingly. "What if I told you that you may never totally get him out of your head?" he asked, his brows arched questioningly.

Mina tore herself from his grasp in frustration. Turning and walking away from him, she cried, "Then we may never make love!"

"I'm not saying it's going to be easy," Jake said, going to grasp her by the arm and turning her back around to face him. "You do this the same way you did everything else in life after losing Keith. You do it one step at a time. Just like you got up every day after he died and kept living. Maybe I won't be the one you make love to. But, one day, you *will* make love again, Mina. You'll know when the time is right."

His eyes devoured her face.

"You'll look at that lucky guy," he said softly, "and he'll look at you, and suddenly it will feel so natural that there won't be anything preventing you from giving and taking pleasure once more."

Mina watched his mouth as he spoke. His square, unshaven jaw, so masculine. His lips so kissable, and when he smiled, his white teeth gleamed in his dark face. Her heart seemed to plummet to the pit of her stomach, and she had never felt more attracted to him than at that moment.

He kept talking, and she closed her eyes as his deep voice washed over her. And his words resonated deep inside of her. It was like a sensual spirit descending on her, soaking into her skin and making her tingle all over.

"Making love isn't all about the release," he said. "It's about sharing your feelings with someone you care about. So I suggest you wait, Mina. Wait until you feel a compulsion to bare yourself, all of you, to the bone, and not just your body. Sex isn't worth the effort unless both parties are willing to do that."

Mina opened her eyes and found him still observing her. She took a deep breath, then reached down, grasped the hem of her shirt and pulled it over her head. "You're that guy, Jake," she said, sounding sure of herself. Her eyes were also determined. Jake could see the difference in her, and his heartbeat accelerated upon seeing it.

He held up his hands in a gesture of surrender. "I'm yours to command."

Mina smiled at that and went to him, pulling him down for a soulful kiss. Jake took her fully into his embrace, and Mina literally climbed his tall, muscular body until she had her legs wrapped around his waist, and he was cupping her behind.

Jake walked like this from the living room back to his bedroom and through the bedroom to the en-suite bath. There, he set her down and began to methodically peel her clothing from her toned yet voluptuous body. Mina let him, reveling in his touch. And when she stood entirely naked in front of him, she didn't avert her eyes. She looked boldly into his and smiled. No, this was not easy to do, as Jake had said, but she did it because she genuinely wanted him, and she would not be hampered by her thoughts any longer. *I love you, Keith. I'll always love you. But I like this man a lot, and I trust him.*

For a moment, Jake held his breath, afraid to make any sudden movements in case this was a dream and it would vanish right before his eyes. Her beauty exceeded his expectations. He'd known she was fit, but her body was also ultrafeminine to him. She had curves where a woman should have curves—her breasts and hips, especially. And she also had muscles. Her arms and legs were sculpted from physical labor. Her skin was like honey all over, but she was not unmarred. She had the occasional scar. He had his share, too.

"You're so beautiful," Jake breathed huskily.

Mina smiled at him and said, "You're still dressed."

Jake laughed and began undressing. "Sorry, I got distracted."

This time it was Mina's turn to enjoy the show. Jake's muscles flexed in his arms, legs and chest as he pulled various articles of clothing from his tall body while Mina had to mentally hold herself back from touching him. Jake was every inch a man to be reckoned with. She sighed. She'd always admired him clothed. In jeans he was a god. She'd seen him in a suit and had to adjust her opinion, giving top honors to that look. But, honestly, being stark naked was his best look, hands down.

The word *beautiful* was not descriptive enough for the way his broad chest, arms, stomach, legs, thighs and butt all came together in one unforgettable masculine package. And she wasn't referring to huge muscles, either, because he didn't have a bodybuilder's form. He was simply in great shape from running and working hard every day. Mina thought bodybuilders moved awkwardly, whereas Jake was poetry in motion.

He stood smiling at her, naked as the day he'd been born.

For a moment Mina stood transfixed, just admiring him. She must have stared too long because Jake said, a bit insistently, "Mina?"

"Just enjoying the view," she said, laughing as she threw her arms around his neck. "You're gorgeous, Jake Wolfe!"

"You had me going there," he teased as he repeatedly kissed her face. "I've been working out extra in anticipation of this day."

Mina had to smile at that admission. It was good to know women weren't the only ones worried about body image.

Jake gestured to the tub. "A bath or a shower?" he asked.

"Shower," Mina answered.

"You're not afraid of getting your hair wet?"

"I'm part mermaid," Mina joked. "I love getting wet."

She proved it by stepping under the spray and allowing the water to drench her from head to foot. Jake soaped a thick washcloth and gently rubbed it all over her. Mina couldn't help softly sighing as he caressed her body.

Mina, in turn, rubbed his body down and relished every moment. Her hands lingered in the hair on his chest. Jake playfully made his pectorals jump underneath her hands, and she laughed softly. "Handsome *and* talented," she quipped.

Jake bent low and, cupping her face in his hands, looked deeply into her eyes. Smiling that killer smile of his, he said, "Mina, do you know what you've done to me?"

Mina rose on her tiptoes and planted a kiss on his chin. "No, tell me."

"You've changed my life. When I wake up, you're my first thought, and when I go to bed, you're my last. You've gotten under my skin, girl."

"That sounds painful," Mina said, feeling delighted and scared all at once. She was happy she was on his mind so much, but was afraid of what that meant.

"It is sometimes," Jake continued, still smiling dreamily. "In this crazy world you take a risk every time you let down your guard and allow someone into your heart. Love can mean loss. We both know that. But there is no love without risk. And I don't know about you, but I'd rather risk my heart and love rather than go without."

Then he kissed her, and there was no going back from that point. They stepped from the shower stall and patted themselves dry, with Jake taking a few minutes to towel dry Mina's braids, and then they moved to the bedroom where more kissing and caressing ensued until they collapsed onto the king-size bed.

They lay on their sides, saying nothing, just gazing into each other's eyes for a moment as they caught their breaths.

Then Jake pulled Mina against his body, and his warmth radiated into her warmth. He bent his head and took one of her nipples into his mouth, and his tongue licked and teased. Intense pleasure shot through Mina. The slow burn that had been flickering inside her for the past half hour of their playful interlude in the shower now turned into a blaze.

Jake smiled devilishly. She was very responsive. He would try another test of her responsiveness. After showing equal attention to her other breast, he got up onto his knees, straddled her and bent his head to rain kisses down her flat stomach while Mina's body ripened under his efforts. He noticed she'd opened her legs further, and he took this as an invitation.

He thrust his face between her legs, luxuriating in the feminine scent of her. When his tongue sought and found her clitoris, he steeled himself for a negative reaction. But she surprised him, and let go and relaxed. He paused for a moment and breathed a sigh of relief, his hot breath inducing Mina even more to let go of her inhibitions and let nature take its course.

He plunged in, and within minutes had Mina writhing on the bed, calling his name. "Jake, Jake, don't stop. No, *stop,* I can't take anymore. Wait, don't stop!"

Jake had no intention of stopping until she was fully satisfied. When that moment came, she screamed his name even louder, and he kissed the insides of her quivering thighs.

Then he got up and put on a condom. Returning to her, he bent and kissed her belly, and pulled her toward him on the bed. Mina was still coming down from her high and was in a mellow state of mind. She grinned crookedly and opened wide. Jake grinned, too, and pressed the tip of his hardened member against the opening of her vagina. Mina raised her hips and took Jake gently. She was tight and hot and wet, and when he finally slid into her up to the hilt, he couldn't help groaning loudly with pleasure. She was everything he'd imagined she'd be, and he'd imagined she'd be wonderful many times.

Soon they achieved a sweet rhythm of give-and-take. Mina was strong. She was not content to lie there and accept his thrusts. Eventually, she wound up on top, and this position gave Jake as much pleasure as it gave her because he got to watch her enjoying herself. She rode him hard, her full breasts doing an up-and-down dance that he could have watched all night long.

When Mina threw her head back, thrust her breasts and her pelvis forward and began chanting, "Oh, God, oh, God," Jake knew she was coming again. He could hold on no longer. He came, hard and fierce.

Mina collapsed onto his broad chest. She smiled at him. "I think it's safe to say we're compatible."

Jake put his arms around her and turned to kiss her forehead. "We fit like a glove."

His tone was light, but his thoughts were anything but. He'd known that he was falling in love with Mina before now, but tonight had confirmed it for him. He had no doubt that he loved her. He didn't believe she was ready to hear it, though. So he remained silent.

They simply held each other, both of them lost in their own thoughts. Then Jake broke the silence with, "Are you hungry? I'm ravenous. How would you like an omelet?"

"Sounds good," Mina returned, sounding altogether too comfortable at this moment to move a muscle.

Chapter 13

"Oh, God, what are you doing to me?" Mina moaned in ecstasy. It had been three days since Mina had returned with him to Atlanta. She was lying on her stomach, and Jake was massaging her lower back, working his way up to her shoulders. His big hands were warm and gentle, but strong. Mina melted at his touch. Her mind hovered somewhere between bliss and sexual stimulation. She could feel her muscles relaxing, but her feminine center was throbbing with erotic intensity.

"I'm trying to take your mind off leaving," Jake said languidly.

Jake, naked except for a towel around his waist, was leaning over her, working magic with his fingers. It was early evening, and they were in the bedroom of his apartment.

Granger had been so pleased with the outcome of the case, and especially Jake's plugging the leak in the agency, that he told Jake not to come into the office for two weeks. Jake had been happy to oblige.

They hadn't ventured far from his bedroom since then.

"I'm not on vacation," Mina reminded him. "I have to get back to Cherokee. They need me."

"I need you," Jake said, then stopped massaging her and sat down on the bed beside her. Mina got up and went into his arms. Looking deeply into his eyes, she said, "That's sweet. I miss you when we're not together, too. And it's been wonderful making up for lost time. But I can't let my grandpa down. I told him I'd only be away for four days. He's getting too old to run the lodge by himself."

Jake sighed with resignation. His golden eyes raked over her face. He loved everything about it, those gorgeous dark eyes that contrasted so nicely with her honey-toned skin. Her high cheekbones. She had a dimple in her chin that appeared when she grinned infectiously. Her mouth tasted like strawberries and cream to him.

"Okay, I'll stop trying to bribe you to stay. We'd better get ready for dinner, then."

Mina smiled at him and briefly kissed his mouth. "I'm looking forward to meeting Leo."

"But first," Jake said, rising and letting the towel around his waist fall to the floor, "I want you one more time."

Mina happily went into his arms and Jake picked her up, cupping her bottom in his hands. She wrapped her legs around him and kissed him. Jake sat down on the bed. Mina reached for a condom from the nightstand, tore it open and rolled it onto his engorged penis.

A moment later, she was on her back and he was pushing inside of her. She arched her back until he filled her all the way up.

They maintained eye contact throughout, each enjoying the looks of pleasure in the other's gazes. "You're a very sensual woman, Mina. Did you know that?"

"I never really gave it much thought," she panted. "To be honest, my mind sort of leaves me when I'm making love to you. It's kind of like an out-of-body experience."

Jake smiled and delved deeper. His hands were cupping her butt, bringing her even closer. "I see what you mean," he murmured.

Mina's thrusts grew more urgent. She was almost there. He was hitting just the right spot, which made her want to open her legs wider and give it up to him. She was his, only his to take. Every nerve ending associated with pleasure in her body was on fire. "I'm yours," she breathed.

Jake bent and kissed her as he came. Mina's legs were wrapped around him, her thrusts coming faster and faster. When she felt Jake throbbing inside of her, she convulsed, too, and an orgasm spread through her until she was trembling in Jake's arms.

"That's good," Jake softly said in her ear. "Because I am definitely yours."

Mina floated on a cloud of sexual satisfaction as she looked deeply into his eyes. *This man is so intense,* she thought. *He's unafraid of his emotions and gives me all of himself every time we're together. Is he this perfect, or am I so sexually fulfilled, I'm not seeing clearly? Why can't I just enjoy myself and stop analyzing everything?*

Jake must have felt the change in her because he gave her a quizzical look and asked, "What's the matter?"

"I'm kind of nervous about meeting Leo," she told him, which was partially true. She couldn't tell him she was suffering from self-doubt because she didn't want to destroy his image of her as the confident, together person he believed her to be. Let him hang onto his illusions this soon in their love affair.

He smiled at her. "I did tell you we're twins, didn't I?"

She gaped at him. "No, you didn't. You just said you had a brother named Leonidas, Leo for short."

"My mistake," he said breezily. "We're so different, I hardly ever think of us as twins. You'll see. We're complete opposites."

Mina could have slapped Jake in anger when Leo walked up to them outside of Bone's, the steakhouse on Piedmont Road, where they'd agreed to meet for their 8:00 p.m. dinner reservation.

She felt like a deer caught in headlights, she was so startled by their resemblance. She had to reach out and grasp Jake's arm to maintain her sense of equilibrium as she stared at a man who was his exact double, except with a bald head. And when Leo opened his mouth to speak, it was like stereo because he also sounded like Jake.

"Mina?" he said, the smile never leaving his face. "My knucklehead brother obviously didn't prepare you for our first meeting." He took Mina's hand and covered it with his own. Mina stared up at him.

She felt slightly dizzy as she took in the golden eyes, strong jaw, sexy dimples and, wait, *perfect nose*. Jake's had been broken once in a fight, he'd told her.

"No, he definitely did not explain himself well enough," she told Leo, feeling more herself now. She took his arm and let go of Jake's. Smiling up at Leo, she said, "I think I like you better."

Leo chuckled and gave his brother a smug look. "A woman with good taste."

They were all dressed for an elegant night on the town, the men in dark suits and Mina in a little red dress and strappy black-suede sandals with four-inch heels. She tossed her long braids behind her as she and Leo strode into the restaurant. Jake followed close behind, a satisfied smile on his lips.

After they were seated, with Mina between the nearly mirror images that were Jake and Leo, Leo looked at Jake and said, "She's too good for you."

Jake smiled lovingly at Mina. "I know, but she likes me anyway."

"Let me see what I can do about changing that tonight," Leo said. He regarded Mina. "Did he tell you he was born first, and when he was being born, he kicked me in the face? He was rude from the beginning, and he only got worse as the years wore on.

"When we were seven he decided that he could drive, so he stole the keys to the family car, and when our parents weren't looking he got behind the wheel, started it, threw it into reverse. He mowed down the mailbox, damaged a neighbor's car and would have plowed into a neighbor's living room if our dad hadn't gotten there in time."

Mina was laughing so hard there were tears in her eyes. "And to think that, until now, I thought you were perfect," she said to Jake, who was smiling.

"I was an active child," he said in his defense.

"He was a menace," Leo said. He reached over and grasped Mina's hand. "But all jokes aside, he turned out all right. For a while there I thought he'd become a hit man or something along those lines."

"Well," Mina said, "they do say that people who can think like a criminal make the best law enforcement officers."

"True," Leo said, looking at his brother with a critical eye. He sighed. "But enough about my pitiful brother. I want to know all about you, Mina. Jake gave me the condensed version. And frankly, I thought he was lying. He made you sound like Wonder Woman—or her darker sister."

Mina smiled at Jake. "He tends to exaggerate when

he talks about me. I'm just an ex-army girl from Raleigh, North Carolina, who's now helping her grandfather run his lodge in the Great Smoky Mountains. How about you, Leo? Jake's told me practically nothing about you." She glared at Jake for his omission. He had the grace to look remorseful.

Leo gave him a baleful glance, as well, before telling Mina, "I'm not surprised he didn't tell you much about me, since at this point in your relationship he's trying to put his best foot forward. You see, Mina, my brother is jealous of my success."

"You teach *literature* at a private girls' school," Jake said.

"I'm molding the minds of future leaders of America," Leo objected. "Women who graduate from Spelman go on to become leaders, real movers and shakers."

"Spelman," Mina said admiringly. She batted her eyelashes at Leo in a playful manner.

"See?" Leo said to Jake. "She's putty in my hands now. And that, my dear Mina, is why Jake's jealous of me. The ladies love a man who respects women."

Their waiter came to take their orders at that point, and conversation came to an abrupt end for the moment. Leo insisted on treating them and ordered a fine pinot noir to complement the steaks that he and Jake ordered, and Mina's crab cakes with corn, roasted red pepper and ginger vinaigrette.

Throughout the evening, Leo regaled Mina with stories about his and Jake's childhood, first in Florida and then in the Bronx. In her mind's eye, Mina could see Jake as he grew from a boy into the man he was, and she was grateful to Leo for that. His vision of his brother, while admittedly biased, was so lovingly vivid that it made her like Jake all the more.

Over dessert—warm pecan pie with praline sauce and French-vanilla ice cream, which Mina shared with Jake—Jake told his brother, "Mina has four sisters. Well, one is married and about to have her first child, but can you imagine that there are three more like her at home?"

Mina knew he was joking, but she honestly thought it was sweet of him to admire her sisters enough to try to entice his single brother with the mention of them.

Leo swallowed a mouthful of chocolate cake and put down his fork. "Wait a minute. You said you were from Raleigh, right?"

Mina nodded. "Yes, most of my family still lives there."

"I'm being courted by Duke, a university in that area," Leo told her. "It's not far from Raleigh, is it?"

Mina smiled. "Duke's in Durham, about thirty minutes away from Raleigh," she answered. "My sister, Lauren, the married one, got her architectural degree from Duke."

"Well, I'm thinking of going for an interview at Duke next month," Leo said, picking up his fork again and cutting off a piece of chocolate cake with the side of it. "I love Spelman, but at this point in my life, I'm open to a change in my routine. Every few years you need to shake things up a little."

"Maybe Meghan would be willing to show Leo the area while he's there," Jake suggested.

Mina knew he'd chosen Meghan because she was also an academic. But some people didn't like to be set up on blind dates. Mina smiled at Leo. "Don't think that you're obligated to have one of my sisters show you around just because Jake suggested it."

"Mina, if your sisters are half as charming as you are, I'd be honored to meet them," Leo said.

So, after their meal, as they stood outside of the restaurant saying their goodbyes, Mina gave Leo her cell phone number, and they promised to keep in touch.

In the car, heading back to his apartment, Mina placed her hand on Jake's thigh and squeezed. "You were right. You're *so* different from each other." She peered at him. "Now I know what you'll look like in a few years when you lose your hair."

Jake chuckled. "I'm not going to react to that dig, Ms. Gaines, because the thought of you and I still being together a few years from now is such a wonderful prospect." And he took her hand with his free one and squeezed it affectionately.

Mina sighed and relaxed on the supple leather seat of the SUV. She was envisioning them together years from now. Her parents and her grandparents had all remained faithful to each other, her parents for more than thirty years, and her grandparents until her grandmother's death. She believed she had it in her to weather whatever storms might arise, and Jake certainly seemed to be the hero type, which meant he'd probably make a great husband and father, the only type of hero she wanted.

She smiled at Jake and said, "Thanks for bringing me tonight. I like Leo, and meeting him only made me like you more."

Jake said softly, "Mina, that's all I wanted to happen tonight. That you'd like my brother, who's my best friend, and that you'd get to know me better as a result. I can feel the reluctance in you to let go and believe in what's happening between us. That it's as good as it feels. And I understand that, really I do. I don't want to rush you. But I have to be honest with you. *I love you.* I *know* this. I have no doubt about it. I'm not telling you now because I want to hear you say the words to me. Know this—I only want to hear you say you love me when you really mean it. And not in the throes of passion or any other time some people toss those words around. Because I don't just want a hot and heavy affair with you, I want it all. Marriage and babies and forever."

Mina took his hand and raised it to her lips, kissing it. "I won't," she promised. "I won't lead you on, Jake. I'll only say the words when I'm sure of myself and I'm ready to do something about it."

"That's my girl," Jake said with a smile.

Mina let go of his hand, and he turned his full attention to his driving.

Inside, Mina was happy to know Jake loved her. To be loved was the greatest blessing that could be bestowed on human beings, in her opinion. But until she could return his love wholeheartedly and without

reservation, she owed it to him be honest. And while
she craved him sexually and liked him as a person,
she had loved only one man, and that was Keith. She
still wasn't sure if she could risk her heart again, even
though she sincerely wanted to be able to. Someday.

For his part, Jake thought the evening had gone
well. As he'd told Mina, he didn't want her love based
on sympathy or because he could make her body sing.
He was looking for something lasting, and he would
hold out for it, no matter how long it took. He wanted
Mina in his life forever, but if Mina didn't believe in
them, he would have no choice but to give her up.
Was she as broken as she sometimes seemed? Or was
she making her way back up to the surface, soon to
break free of the bonds that were holding her back
from loving again? He was rooting for her. He was
rooting for *them*.

When they got back to his apartment, he carried
her to the bedroom and they made love fiercely, as
though this were their last time. He wondered at the
emotions that swirled around that room, threatening to consume them. The power they possessed as
a couple was palpable. He believed in it, and with
every thrust he tried to communicate that feeling
to Mina.

From her reaction, the most sumptuously erotic
experience he'd ever had with her, he was optimistic
that they'd pulled apart some of the chains that bound
her broken heart.

Spent, they fell asleep in each other's arms. Jake

was satiated with his thoughts on their future. Mina ardently reached for him as she drifted into a dream-filled sleep. And he pulled her snugly against his warm body.

Chapter 14

"Grandpa, I'm home!" Mina called as she unlocked the front door and strode into the cabin she shared with her grandfather.

Jake was right behind her, carrying her bags. Mina sniffed the air. It smelled like someone had prepared breakfast that morning. The aroma of fresh coffee and the enticing smell of bacon lingered.

Suddenly she heard the crash of a dish breaking on the kitchen floor. She and Jake hurried in that direction, Jake pausing long enough to place her bags on the foyer floor.

Mina was surprised to find Miss Mabel in the kitchen wearing an apron over a nightgown, her feet in slippers, looking just as surprised to see *her*.

"Mina, you're home," Miss Mabel cried in astonishment. Mina felt sorry for her because it was apparent that she was embarrassed that she had been caught in her sleepwear. Mina was stunned into silence as she watched Miss Mabel hastily clean up the broken pieces of a plate and deposit them in the trash.

Before Mina could utter a word, her grandfather, who must have heard both her yelling for him and the sound of the dish breaking, came barreling into the kitchen wearing only his pajamas. His wavy snow-white hair was in disarray, as if he'd just gotten out of bed.

Mina wasn't naive. Her grandfather and Miss Mabel were more than friends. "I'm sorry," she said to both of them. "I should have called and told you we were on our way."

Miss Mabel clutched the top of her robe as she made a hasty exit, saying, "I'm going to get dressed." Her dark brown eyes sought Benjamin's as she left. Benjamin gave an almost imperceptible nod.

"Well, I reckon it's time I explained Mabel's and my relationship," he said in resignation.

Mina smiled. "It's none of my business, Grandpa. Did you imagine I thought you'd been celibate all these years, a healthy man like you?"

Benjamin walked over and poured himself a cup of coffee. He looked up. "Would you two join me?"

"I can wait in the other room…" Jake began.

Benjamin laughed. "You can stay, Jake. I'm not gonna say anything you can't hear."

So the three of them sat down at the kitchen table with mugs of freshly brewed coffee in front of them, whereupon Benjamin looked at Mina and began talking. "Mabel and I have been a couple for five years now. I knew when I hired her that she was my type, big, boisterous and full of life, just like your grandmother. But I figured I was too old for her. I've got twenty years on her, so I avoided her for the first four years she was here. But one day she came to me and told me how she felt about me, and I confessed I felt the same, and from that day on we've been keeping company."

Mina was smiling and nodding. "I knew Miss Mabel was sweet on you, but you never let on, Grandpa."

"In my day, we kept things like affairs under wraps. I didn't want people getting the wrong idea about Mabel. She's a good woman, but even good women have needs and shouldn't have to endure gossip in order to satisfy them," Benjamin explained. "This is a small town, and people talk."

"Besides," Mabel said, coming back into the kitchen, fully dressed, "I asked Ben not to say anything about us until I was ready to break the news to my children. I know they're grown, but they have certain ideas about how their mother should conduct her private business."

Benjamin smiled at her and got up to pull the other chair at the kitchen table out for her. "Can I get you some coffee?" he asked sweetly.

"Yes, thank you," Mabel said as she sat down. Her long salt-and-pepper hair, thick and natural, lay in a single braid down her back, and her brown skin with red undertones glowed. Mina thought she looked lovely.

She and Mina looked at one another and burst out laughing. "I'm sorry I scared you, Miss Mabel."

"Honey, I'm just glad it was only a plate I broke and not my leg. I was in such a rush to get out of here."

Benjamin returned with Mabel's cup of coffee and handed it to her. "Thank you, dear," said Mabel.

Mina couldn't stop smiling. Her grandfather and Miss Mabel were so adorable to watch. She could see by the warmth in their eyes when they looked at each other that there was genuine affection there, quite possibly love.

Then a thought occurred to her. "Does Mom know?" she asked her grandfather as he sat back down at the table.

Benjamin shook his head. "No, but she soon will, because Mabel and I got married yesterday."

Mina gaped at them. "Oh, my God," she exclaimed happily. "Congratulations, you two!"

Mabel blushed like a young bride. Benjamin draped an arm around her. "I told her I'm not worth much as a husband, but she loves me anyway. A man can't ask for more than that."

"Oh, you," Mabel said, pooh-poohing his disparaging remarks. "You're a catch, and you know it!"

"I want to be there when you tell Mom," Mina said as she hugged her grandfather, then her new step-grandmother.

"Then you'll get your wish because we're having

Thanksgiving here this year, and your folks are coming. Mabel and I will make the announcement then."

Mina thought Mabel looked a little nervous. But then her mother, Virginia, made a lot of people nervous. She gave Mabel another affectionate squeeze and said, "Let me be the first to welcome you to the family, Miss Mabel, um, what am I supposed to call you now?"

Mabel grinned. "Oh, child, just call me what you've always called me."

"That doesn't seem appropriate now," Mina good-naturedly disagreed. "How about Nana? I've always wanted a Nana."

"I've never been anyone's Nana before," said Mabel, trying on the label for size. "I like it."

"Nana it is!" cried Mina, and kissed Mabel's cheek.

Jake noticed that his coworkers regarded him as a hero when he returned to work. So many people came up to him to congratulate him on busting Charlie Betts and inadvertently ferreting out the mole that he was beginning to feel self-conscious. After all, in his estimation, it had only been dumb luck. It was amazing that he and Mina were still alive, let alone around to receive kudos.

He said as much to Granger, the morning he got back from his vacation.

Granger, a Blow Pop in his hand, the latest prop in his endless quest to quit smoking, laughed at Jake's modesty. "Jake, luck doesn't figure into it. If you were not a trained agent with skills, you and Ms. Gaines wouldn't be here." He sat down behind his desk after gesturing for Jake to sit. "You know, I looked into her background."

He took out a folder and began to skim it. "Says here that she was honorably discharged from the army a couple of years ago. Her record was impressive. She made captain in six years. Flew countless missions into combat zones and rescued hundreds of soldiers. Before the army, she excelled at the military academy she attended. Won medals in sharpshooting and hand-to-hand combat. She sounds like a female Rambo." He glanced at a photo of Mina that was in the file. "Good-looking gal, too," he added.

Jake was a little irritated by the last comment. "And you're saying all of this because…?"

"I was wondering if she'd consider coming to work for us," said Granger.

"I already suggested it, and she flatly refused." Jake was happy to tell Granger this. He'd had some time to reconsider his stance on Mina joining the DEA. She seemed happy where she was, and her happiness was more important to him than having her join his team.

"Mmm," said Granger contemplatively. "Too bad, we could use someone like her."

Hoping to end the conversation, Jake asked, "Am I going to be assigned another case soon?"

The Betts case was wrapped up, as far as the agency was concerned. Charlie Betts was in the hospital recuperating from being kicked by a horse. He'd sustained a head injury, two broken ribs and a fractured jaw. It was a miracle he was alive. Former Special Agent Neil Olsen had confessed his part in the matter and was asking for leniency, which the agency was considering if he agreed to testify against his cousin. Testimony or no testimony, he would definitely spend time in prison; how much time depended on how useful his testimony turned out to be.

For aiding Charlie Betts in luring Jake to what could have proved to be his death, Mario Fuentes would probably have more years tacked onto his eventual sentence.

"How do you feel about becoming Special Agent in Charge of the Greensboro, North Carolina office?" asked Granger. He pushed the Blow Pop into his mouth and sucked on it furiously while waiting for Jake's reaction to his question.

He didn't have to wait long. Jake already knew that Greensboro was nearly three hundred miles from Cherokee. He'd be closer to Mina if he were in Atlanta. "Not too good," he stated plainly. "I'd prefer to stay in Atlanta, if it's all the same to you."

"It means a promotion," Granger said encouragingly. "And a significant hike in pay."

Jake still shook his head. "That's tempting, sir, but I'm going to have to decline."

Frowning, Granger asked, "Why?"

"I've given this agency ten years of my life," Jake said. "During which time I've never refused an assignment, and I've performed to the best of my abilities each and every time. My reasons for declining are personal."

Granger sat up straighter in his chair, his expression going from confused to resigned. "Yes, you have been an exemplary agent. All right, Jake. Then I suppose I'll have to find another assignment for you. I'll contact you once things are finalized."

Jake rose. "Thank you, sir."

Granger nodded. His face was somber. As Jake left, he wondered if Granger was disappointed he hadn't jumped at the opportunity to head the Greensboro field office. But he was determined to stick by his decision. He felt he'd earned the right to turn down an assignment if it didn't suit him.

Mina was in the barn feeding carrots and apples to Cinnamon, Midnight and the other two horses one afternoon when her grandfather walked in.

She was standing at Midnight's stall. The mare seemed calmer these days. Mina wondered if she sensed that her future hung in the balance after she'd struck a human, albeit not a very nice human. Did horses understand more than humans thought they did?

Benjamin joined her at the stall. "You know we're going to have to sell her."

"I know," Mina said. "You can't have her around the guests if there's a possibility that she'll kick someone else. But do you think anyone will want her, given her past?"

Benjamin nodded. "Experienced horse people will know how to handle her. It's just that a lot of our guests are greenhorns. We can't take the risk."

Mina affectionately patted Midnight's huge head. The horse looked at her with her beautiful, intelligent brown eyes. Only a few hours after the incident in the woods, Midnight and Cinnamon had found their way home. Chad had spotted them wandering the tree line adjacent to the lodge and brought them to the barn, fed them, gave them fresh water and rubbed them down.

"I'm going to miss you, girl," Mina said softly. "You saved my life, and I'm not going to forget it."

Later that night, Mina lay in bed with the phone pressed to her ear. Jake was telling her about his day, and she was listening raptly. It had been two weeks since he'd brought her back to Cherokee after her short visit to Atlanta.

"Got my new assignment today," he told her. "I'm going undercover again, this time in Tennessee."

"Which city?" Mina asked. "Or can you tell me?"

"Chattanooga," Jake answered.

"That's not far from me at all," Mina happily noted.

"I know," said Jake. "I'll sneak away to see you as often as possible."

Mina sobered. "You will be extra careful?"

Jake laughed softly. "Baby, I'm always extra careful."

"Yes, Jake, I understand that, but having seen firsthand what your work entails, I still worry about you."

Jake changed the subject and told her about Granger's desire to recruit her.

Mina laughed at that. "I was safer in Afghanistan,"

she said. "My life has been threatened more often in the past month than in six years of military service."

"I told him you weren't interested," Jake said quietly.

Mina thought she detected a note of relief in his voice. "You sound pleased that I'm not interested," she said. "You were trying to recruit me not too long ago."

"That was before I fell in love with you," Jake told her. "If you remember, we barely knew each other at that point. I was just making conversation, trying to impress you."

"Dating games, huh?" Mina said with a smile.

"I was complimenting you on your accomplishments and showing an interest in you," Jake explained. "While not knowing much about you. But after knowing you for a while, I can see you're really not interested in becoming an agent."

"So, Chattanooga," Mina said. "How soon do you begin the assignment?"

"I'm already here," Jake told her.

"You're not after someone as dangerous as Charlie Betts, are you?"

"You know I can't discuss the case, but these guys are small-time compared to Betts, if that's what you're worried about."

"That doesn't make them any less dangerous," Mina insisted.

"Mina, let it go and tell me you miss me."

"I miss you!"

"I miss you, too. I'll try to drop by soon, can't say when."

"Anytime is a good time," Mina told him. She sighed. "Good night, sweetie."

"Good night," Jake said.

After she hung up the phone, Mina got comfortable in bed, turned off the lamp on the nightstand and settled down.

As soon as she closed her eyes, her cell phone rang. Picking it up, she checked the display. It was an Atlanta number, but there was no name listed. She smiled as she quickly picked up the call before the phone stopped ringing. "Hello, this is Mina."

"Mina," said Leo Wolfe, sounding as though he was smiling. "This is Leo."

Mina knew it was Leo because he sounded just like Jake. She sat up in bed and turned the lamp on again. "Hi, Leo, how are you?"

"I'm well," he said. "I'm calling to let you know I'll be visiting Durham this weekend and wondered if you would ask your sister Meghan if she could meet me somewhere for lunch on Saturday."

Mina was excited by the prospect. Meghan was not involved with anyone, and when Mina had told her about Leo, and been sure to mention that Leo and Jake were identical twins, Meghan had been intrigued. "I'll try," she told Leo. "Give me the particulars, and I'll pass on everything to Meghan."

"You can give her my cell phone number," Leo told her. "And if she's interested, she can give me a call. I don't know much about Durham. She might be able to suggest a place to meet."

"All right," said Mina brightly.

Leo went on to tell Mina when he would arrive in Durham and where he would be staying.

When she hung up, she had the spooky feeling that she'd just had another conversation with Jake. Getting used to Leo was going to take some time.

Chapter 15

On Thanksgiving morning, Mina was up at the crack of dawn so that she could put the turkey in the oven and let it cook slowly. She and Miss Mabel were an unbeatable team in the kitchen. Miss Mabel was the kind of cook who was patient and kind to those less talented than she was. Mina, who had never prepared a Thanksgiving feast before, learned a lot from her.

Miss Mabel, who was nervous about the announcement she and Ben were going to make today, appreciated Mina's sense of humor about the situation.

"Look, Nana," Mina said respectfully to her while they were cooking together in the kitchen that morning, "it makes no difference what my mother's opinion is about you and Grandpa getting married. Grandpa chose you, and that's what counts. Mom doesn't have anything to say about it!"

"It's not as if I've never met the rest of the family," Mabel said reasonably as she chopped celery for the stuffing. "I've met them all, just not as your grandfather's bride."

"Everything's going to be fine," Mina tried to reassure her.

"Unless something happens," Mabel said pessimistically.

"No, we're not having any of that," Mina chided her. "Repeat after me. Everything's going to be fine."

"Everything's going to be fine," Mabel said, forcing a smile that didn't quite reach her eyes.

Mina let it go. She understood doubt. She suffered from it herself, and no amount of cheerleading could dispel it. You had to believe in yourself. She was learning that every day, and she was growing more confident.

She closed her eyes for a moment as she rinsed sweet potatoes at the sink and envisioned the whole family at the dinner table this afternoon, including Jake, who had told her he would try to make it, but to forgive him if he was absent. Since he'd gone undercover in Chattanooga, he'd been able to slip away to come see her once. And thanks to the fact that her grandfather now spent his nights at his new bride's house, she and Jake had been able to get some alone time together.

She sighed. Loving a man of action was hard sometimes. She caught herself, heart thudding. Did she just think *love?* Had falling in love with Jake sneaked up on her? Smiling, she let herself go and admitted it. Yes, she loved him!

She wanted to shout it out, but turning to glance at Miss Mabel, who was serenely chopping celery, she didn't think this was the right time for that. She turned off the water. The sweet potatoes could wait. "Be right back," she murmured to Miss Mabel as she quickly left the kitchen and went to her bedroom to phone Jake and see if he was on the way.

Sitting on the bed, she picked up the cell phone from the nightstand, its usual spot when she wasn't carrying it around with her. Jake didn't pick up. She listened to his voicemail message, enjoying the sound of his rich baritone.

When it was time for her to leave a message, she simply said, "I miss you, you big, beautiful man, you!" She knew she sounded inordinately happy, perhaps like an idiot, but she didn't care. She couldn't tell him she loved him over the phone. That was something that needed to be said face-to-face. So she added, "I hope to see you today, but if I don't, know that you'll be on my mind."

She hung up and let out a disappointed sigh. Then she grinned. She was in love! She'd made the transition from a woman who was fearful of loving anyone after Keith to a woman with trust and faith and hope in her heart. All because she'd pulled a man out of a crashed aircraft—a very special man with the patience and love it required to wait out her fears.

* * *

The Raleigh part of the family arrived at one that afternoon. Her father's black Hummer pulled up first, closely followed by Colton and Lauren's silver Range Rover. Mina went outside to greet them. She was especially happy to see her brother-in-law, Colton, because he hadn't been able to come the last time the family had visited, and it had been months since she'd seen him.

They got out of the cars, all dressed casually in jeans and such, looking healthy and, in Lauren's case, about to burst. She was now eight months along, and the baby could come at any moment. Mina went right to her and Colton.

Lauren's golden-brown skin looked clear and vibrant, and Mina could see she wasn't wearing makeup. She hugged her and peered up into her face. Her sister was a few inches taller than she was. "Girl, you are gorgeous!"

Lauren was smiling widely. "I *feel* gorgeous," she said. "I don't know what it is, Mina. For the past few weeks, except for the obvious discomfort when I'm trying to sleep, I've had so much energy, and the hormones are kicking in, making me feel as if I'm on a mood-altering drug half the time."

Colton, six-three and well built, the epitome of a Southern gentleman, beamed at his wife. "She's nesting. It's like living with an alien," he joked. "She's in a good mood all the time."

Lauren laughed and playfully slugged him on the

arm. "Watch it, buddy, or the old Lauren will make an appearance."

Virginia walked up then and said, with a meaningful glance at Mina, "What, no hug for your mother?"

Mina dutifully bent and gave her mother a tight hug. Straightening, she noticed her father with a huge covered pan in his hands. "Momma, I told you there was no need to bring any food. Miss Mabel and I have it covered."

"Oh, child, it's just a little ham," said Virginia offhandedly. "A twenty-five pounder."

Mina laughed. "Oh, yeah, that's a little ham, all right." But she resolved not to let her mother get to her today. She was in love. Her grandfather and Miss Mabel had their big announcement to make, and she wasn't going to do anything to spoil that. Plus, she still held out hope that Jake would make it here by dessert, at least.

She smiled warmly at her mother and said, "Thanks, Momma. That was very thoughtful of you."

Her mother's eyes stretched in surprise. "You're taking this pretty well. I thought you'd raise a ruckus. I know how cantankerous you can be, sometimes." She peered more closely at Mina. "Is there something you want to tell me, something pertaining to that handsome Jake Wolfe?"

Mina didn't have time to explain to her mother that she wasn't going to allow anything to spoil her day. Not even her mother's insistence on bringing a huge ham to the festivities when Mina had told her that she and Miss Mabel were preparing Thanksgiving dinner.

Meghan and Desiree came to her rescue by pulling their mother away and up the steps to the cabin. "Enough of the inquisition, Mother dear," said Desiree who was, as usual, the only one not in jeans but in a lovely dress. Sometimes Mina envied Desiree's ability to always look impeccably feminine.

"Yeah," Meghan said, winking at Mina. "Give M a break."

Mina smiled. Her sisters always had her back.

The last of the party, her father, burdened with the twenty-five pound ham, bent and kissed her on the cheek. "I can't help it, I'm curious, too. Is Jake coming today?"

"He's going to try to make it," Mina said, "work permitting."

At that moment, in Chattanooga, work wasn't permitting Jake very much leeway. He and his team had the home of Calvin Taylor under surveillance. Presently Taylor, who was responsible for practically half of the drugs dealt on the streets of Chattanooga, was hosting a Thanksgiving dinner for key members of his organization and their families. The DEA didn't make it a habit to raid a house with women and children in it. But they had it on good authority that after the dinner, Taylor and his men would retire to his nightclub a few blocks from his home to give out the yearly bonuses for loyalty.

Right now, Jake and fellow agent Adam Hurston were in a black SUV down the block from Taylor's residence. "What is he, the CEO of crime?" Adam joked about Taylor giving out bonuses for loyalty. "I bet he also gives out frozen turkeys to the community for Christmas."

"I believe he does," said Jake laconically. He, like most of his colleagues, detested stakeouts. But they were a big part of the job. Watching and waiting.

He was in a suit today, but for the past four weeks he'd been associating with several of Taylor's men and had taken on the role of someone desperate to get in on the action. Because drug dealers were notoriously paranoid, it had taken them a while to let down their guard and give him a chance. He also pretended to have a drug problem, so he'd been lax with his hygiene, let his hair get matted, neglected to shave and wore thrift-shop clothes to look the part.

Desmond King, one of Taylor's men, had taken pity on him and let him work as his gofer, taking great pleasure in bossing him around. Jake didn't mind, because during the course of his duties he kept his eyes and ears open, and that's how he'd found out about the tradition of Taylor throwing a huge Thanksgiving dinner at his home every year for his chosen people, then afterward hosting a party with strippers at his club where he gave out bonuses. It had been a stroke of luck. A stroke of luck that would, Jake hoped, result in a string of arrests and the end of his sojourn in Chattanooga.

To Mina's relief, Miss Mabel was warmly greeted by the entire family. Mina saw her grandfather's new wife relax a little as they sat down to dine, with Miss

Mabel sitting on one side of her grandfather at the table and Virginia, who was very proprietary of her father, on the other.

Mina sat between Desiree and Meghan, and while everyone was eating and chatting, she took the opportunity to ask Meghan how her lunch date with Leo had gone. Mina was dying to know. She'd wanted to phone and ask days ago, but she figured if Meghan wanted to talk about it, she would call *her*. And she didn't want to call Leo and ask him, for fear she'd appear to be a busybody.

So she peered at her youngest sister now and softly asked, "Meg, what did you think of Leo?"

Meghan looked startled by the question. Mina's heart sank. It must not have gone well. "Oh, no, something went wrong?"

Meghan looked sheepish. "I blew it," she said in a low voice. "I absolutely blew it. When we first met, I gawked at him, M. I didn't mean to. And during the meal, I tried to make up for my behavior by talking too much. I'm sure I scared the poor man off. As proof of that, I haven't heard from him since then, and it's been two weeks. It's a shame, too, because after we started talking and I calmed down a bit, I really liked him."

Mina smiled encouragingly. "I'm sure Leo has gone through that sort of thing before. I did tell you how I reacted to seeing them both in the same place, didn't I?"

Meghan nodded. "You told me, but I still wasn't

prepared, and this bothers me so much, M, because I pride myself on treating everyone with respect."

"I'm sure there's a logical explanation why Leo hasn't gotten in contact with you," Mina insisted. She made a mental note to ask Jake if he'd heard from Leo concerning his date with Meghan. Maybe Meghan was fretting over nothing. But fourteen days without a phone call or an email or a text message *was* a long time.

She reached over, grasped Meghan's hand and squeezed it affectionately. "What do you want to do about it?"

"*Do* about it?"

"Do you want to pursue it or let it go? Because if you really like him, I'll get to the bottom of this," Mina told her, a determined expression on her face.

Meghan smiled. "That's sweet of you, sis, but I'm too mortified to pursue it. Leo would have to make the next move, and I sincerely don't believe that's going to happen."

Mina held up her hands in a gesture of defeat. "Okay, I won't mention it again."

"Thank you," said Meghan sincerely. "Honestly, it went that badly."

Mina continued eating. She looked around the table. Her mother and Miss Mabel were talking about something that was making Miss Mabel smile awkwardly. She wished she could hear what they were saying. Her grandfather, sitting between the two women, wore a baleful expression on his weather-beaten face. She noticed he was watching his daughter out of the corner of his eye, a look that Mina was all too familiar with. His daughter was doing something to irritate him.

She saw him take a deep breath, push his chair back and get up. He stepped back and held out his hand to Miss Mabel, who took it and rose also.

He put his arm about her waist and drew her close to his side. "I was going to wait until later to tell you all about Mabel and me, but I think I should go ahead and tell you right now so there will be no misunderstandings." He directed his gaze at his daughter. "Virginia, it's not *sweet* that Mabel and I are such good friends, and you don't need to thank her for keeping an eye on your dotty old father. Mabel and I are in love, and we're married. It's a done deal, and we hope you all will be happy for us."

With that, he kissed Miss Mabel soundly to cheers from everyone in the family except his daughter, who looked as though she were about to explode.

"She's my age!" Virginia bellowed, loudly enough to be heard over the racket.

She succeeded in quieting the room. Satisfied she had everyone's attention, she went on. "She's only after you for one thing, your money. What else could she possibly see in you? You're over eighty!"

"Ginny!" Alfonse cried, appalled by his wife's behavior. "Keep a civil tongue in your head. That's your father you're talking to."

Virginia stared at her husband, her expression unchanging. "I'm trying to protect him from this, this, gold digger!"

Benjamin pulled himself up to his full height, and stepped in front of his daughter. Miss Mabel stayed by his side, head held high. "No, you're trying to protect your inheritance, which is safe. Don't worry about that. As for Mabel being a gold digger, she doesn't need my money. She does quite well for herself and really doesn't need to work here. She just does it to stay busy and to stay close to me."

Miss Mabel smiled at him. She regarded Virginia. "You can speak with my accountant if you wish."

"I'm going to be a kept man," Benjamin joked. "Mabel could buy me ten times over."

"I'll take good care of you, sugar," Miss Mabel cooed.

Mina relished the scene: Miss Mabel looking supremely confident all of a sudden, her mother standing there with her mouth agape—a look of utter confusion on her face—and the rest of them laughing uproariously.

She just wished Jake were here.

Later that night Jake found himself in the middle of chaos—drug dealers being chased around a strip club by DEA agents and the Chattanooga Police SWAT team. Luckily there had been no gunshots fired so far. Jake would later learn that this was due to the fact that Taylor required everyone to check their guns at the door because alcohol, strippers and guns didn't mix, in his opinion.

Now, though, as Jake ran around with the other law-enforcement officers rounding up Taylor's men and handcuffing them, he expected someone to start shooting at any moment.

Finally, he confronted Taylor, who, amazingly, sat in the VIP section of the club the whole time, sipping a rum and Coke, and shaking his head in disgust. Jake, training his gun on him, told him he was under arrest.

"I know you," Taylor, a good-looking African-American guy in his late twenties, said. "You're Desmond's flunky."

Jake nodded. "That's right."

"You clean up well," Taylor complimented him.

Jake could see a weapon in its shoulder holster under Taylor's suit jacket. He hoped he wouldn't have to shoot anyone else. He was already going to a psychologist to talk through his experience with Danny Betts.

"I saw you with your beautiful wife and children earlier," Jake told him. "I don't know about you, but I want to see the woman I love tonight, not end up in the morgue."

Taylor's eyes roamed the room. All of his men had been rounded up at this point and were being led out of the club. "I'm a businessman, not a thug."

He calmly removed his weapon and handed it to Jake. Jake handcuffed him and led him outside, where he turned Taylor over to a police officer.

Adam walked up to him then. "Everything went smoothly," he reported. "Now it's all paperwork."

Jake glanced at his watch. It was 10:20 p.m. If he left now, he would make it to Cherokee at around one in the morning. "You don't mind handling that, do you?" he asked Adam. "I'll owe you one."

Adam chuckled. "All right, MM, I'll take care of things from here."

Jake laughed, too. It didn't seem he was going to live down the birthday-card incident anytime soon.

Chapter 16

Because the lodge was closed for Thanksgiving, the family had the run of the place and everyone bedded down for the night either in the lodge itself or one of the cabins. The result was that Mina had the cabin all to herself. Her grandfather had gone home with his new wife, much to his daughter's disgust. In her discontent, Virginia had tried to force her husband to take her elsewhere for the night, perhaps Harrah's Cherokee Casino Resort, but, Mina was happy to note, her father had flatly refused, saying he wasn't throwing good money after bad just because she was having a hissy fit.

Mina laughed softly now as she settled in bed. What a day!

Her mother had reacted much as Mina had expected she would, but her grandfather and Miss Mabel had stood their ground. And miracle upon miracles, her father had not bent to her mother's will.

Mina picked up the photo of her and Jake that she kept in a silver frame on her nightstand. In it she was standing in front of him, and he had his arms wrapped around her. They were smiling widely, looking like two people in love. She'd checked her messages earlier, and there had been nothing from him. She was trying not to worry, though. The nature of his job sometimes dictated that he wouldn't be in communication with family and friends. She knew this. She knew it, but she was still worried.

Putting the photo back on the nightstand, she laid her head on her pillow and switched off the lamp. The last thing she saw as she drifted to sleep were the green block numbers on the digital clock's display: 12:34 a.m.

Jake arrived on lodge grounds at 1:15 a.m. and recognized the general's black Hummer but not the silver Range Rover. At any rate, with the presence of the cars, he realized that Mina had guests and he would not be able to surprise her the way he'd been planning to. With that plan blown, he dialed her cell phone number as he sat outside her cabin in the idling agency-issued black SUV.

"Mullo?" she slurred.

"Hello, baby," said Jake, laughing softly.

"It's so good to hear your voice," Mina said.

"Sorry I woke you. I hope the ringing didn't disturb your family."

"Are you here?" Mina asked hopefully.

"Yeah, but I was going to go find a hotel and come back tomorrow. It wouldn't be…"

She cut him off. "No, I'm alone in the house. Don't you dare go anywhere," she cried. "I'm going to open the door for you right now!"

Jake smiled. From the sound of her voice, he could tell she really wanted to see him, which warmed his heart and gave him hope that she might be falling in love with him after all. "I'm getting out of the car," he told her.

Mina had her eye to the peephole when he stepped onto the porch, and she swung the door open.

Jake stood outside, looking in, his grin lighting up his whole being. Mina grasped him by the arm and pulled him inside. "What are you waiting for, an invitation?" she joked.

She closed and locked the door, then stared up at him. He knew he looked a little rumpled in his suit pants, dress shirt, loosened tie and black oxfords. He needed a shave, and was surely weary about the eyes from lack of sleep.

"Oh, baby," she moaned before throwing herself into his arms and kissing him with everything she had.

It seemed that they could not get close enough. Frantically, they undressed each other right there in the foyer, talking between impassioned kisses. "Where have you been?" Mina asked.

"Raiding a strip club," he answered.

"Is that part of your job description?"

"A man's gotta do what a man's gotta do," was his reply. He managed a rakish grin before she jumped into his arms and wrapped her strong legs around his waist. Jake carried her down the hall to her bedroom, where they fell onto the bed, both naked, although Jake still had on his socks.

Mina scrambled to get condoms from the nightstand drawer while Jake took the opportunity to remove his socks. Once again giving him her full attention, Mina pushed him onto his back, straddled him and carefully rolled the condom onto his erect penis. This done, she ran her hands over his hard, muscular chest. Jake fairly trembled with pent-up desire. He'd been dreaming of her silken skin, how good she felt, how good she smelled. She was looking at him now with dark, smoldering eyes full of wanton sexual longing. Seeing that look in her eyes made him harder still.

"Not too long ago you told me that you didn't want me to tell you I loved you while I was in the throes of passion," she said softly, her gaze holding his. "Unfortunately I'm going to have to disappoint you because only five minutes after seeing you again, I'm already in the throes of passion."

Jake was looking at her with a confused expression.

"I love you," Mina told him. "I love you!"

Jake pulled her into his arms. "I finally wore you

down," he quipped. Golden-brown eyes looked deeply into dark brown ones. "When did you know?"

She told him about the instant she had known she loved him, and explained that she had probably loved him before then but had simply been unable to recognize it for what it was. "I was living in denial," she said. "Trying to convince myself that if I guarded my heart, I wouldn't get hurt again if I lost you."

"But life doesn't work that way," Jake said. "Happiness is a risk we take every day. There is none without pain."

"And we have to risk pain to get to the happiness part," Mina said with a sigh.

Then their bodies wouldn't let them deny the magnetic pull between them any longer, and she opened her legs to him and he entered her. Once again the pleasure-and-pain principle was manifested in their coupling, the sweet torture of wanting to explode but holding back long enough for the other to experience pleasure first. Then they were in sync, their bodies moving, sliding against one another with an as-yet-unheard-of ferocity.

They spent every ounce of passion on each other, not stopping until they were both panting and in need of the ultimate release. When they came, they came simultaneously, and they both knew the difference between having sex and making love. Making love was much more fulfilling.

Afterward, they lay facing each other and smiling contentedly. "You said that you wouldn't tell me you loved me until you were ready to do something about it," Jake reminded her. "What do you want to do about it?"

"I want the same things you want," Mina told him. "Marriage and kids, the works."

While Jake was listening to Mina with all his heart, his body betrayed him—his stomach growled.

Mina heard it and laughed. "I see you didn't stop to get something to eat on the way here."

"Too anxious to see you," Jake said with his hand on his flat belly.

"I'll fix you a plate," Mina offered, already climbing out of bed. "We've got enough leftovers to last for days."

Jake sat up in bed. "I'll get cleaned up."

"We both will," Mina said.

They showered together, then Mina left him in the bathroom to shave while she went to the kitchen to warm his food in the microwave.

When he entered the kitchen a few minutes later, he found Mina already sitting at the table enjoying a cup of cocoa, and there was a plate of leftover Thanksgiving dinner at his place setting.

Mina looked up and smiled. "Enjoy. Miss Mabel and I prepared most of it. Momma brought the ham, enough to feed an army."

Jake sat down and began eating. Watching Mina and eating. Devouring Mina with his eyes and eating. After half the food was gone, he set his fork down. His appetite for food had been satisfied. His appetite for Mina, he realized, would never be.

And not just in a sexual way. He'd missed talking to her, watching her facial expressions, the way her body moved. She moved like a dancer, fluid and graceful, her body a well-oiled machine.

"Thank you," he said. "That was delicious."

Mina watched him watching her. "You're making me self-conscious," she said. "Is my hair mussed up?"

"Yes, and I love it that way."

Mina touched her hair, which was out of its usual braids and was long and wavy, nappy. She smiled at him. "I used to have it chemically straightened just to control it. Then I realized the chemicals were weakening my hair. Now I let it run wild and free."

"Don't ever go back to straightening it," Jake said fondly. He continued to look at her with so much love in his eyes that Mina blushed with embarrassment.

She searched for a way to distract him from his intense perusal of her. Then she remembered Meghan and Leo. "Jake, did Leo mention his lunch date with Meghan? Meghan thinks she chased him away. She says she reacted badly to how much you two look alike. Okay, what she said was she gawked at him and possibly made him feel like a freak of nature. She's very sorry she behaved that way. In fact, she's so sorry for how she acted, she refuses to contact him ever again and will only speak to him if he makes the first move."

Jake laughed shortly. "You Gaines girls don't know your own power, do you?"

Mina looked at him as though he were speaking Greek, a language she understood about as well as she'd just understood his statement about her and her sisters. "What's that supposed to mean?"

"Leo's smitten with your baby sister," Jake stated plainly.

"You're kidding!"

"I am not," Jake insisted. "He hasn't phoned her because he thinks he's too old for her. He found her to be, his words exactly, 'delightful and untouched by the machinations and designs of most members of the opposite sex.'"

"He sounds just like Meghan," Mina said. "They're definitely college professors. But why would he think he's too old for her? Meghan's twenty-seven."

"Leo has nine years on her."

"My grandfather has twenty on Miss Mabel," Mina reminded him.

"Let me explain Leo," Jake said. "He's a throwback to when men were like the knights of old, chivalrous. He believes those nine years set him and Meghan so far apart that he would be taking advantage of her due to her relative lack of worldly experience. If Meghan wants him, she's going to have to be the one to pursue him. That's just how he is."

"That's ridiculous," said Mina.

"I agree," Jake said. "That doesn't make it any less true, though."

"Then it's all up to Meghan," Mina concluded. "And she won't contact him because she's embarrassed by how she acted."

"Stay out of it, Mina," Jake said gently. "If they're

meant to be, one of them will break down and contact the other."

Mina yawned. "Let's go back to bed."

"Mina, are you going to stay out of it?"

Mina got up and removed his plate from the table, dumped the remains into the trash and washed it, along with her empty cup.

Jake went to stand next to her at the sink. "You're ignoring me," he accused lightly.

"Yes, I am, because I know my sister just like you know your brother, and they aren't going to get together unless someone does something. They're both old-fashioned geeks."

Jake waited the few seconds it took her to put the dishes she'd washed in the dish rack and dry her hands on a dish towel before pulling her into his arms. "I've got an idea. We can have them in our wedding party. They'll have to see each other at least two times, at the rehearsal and at the wedding."

Mina smiled up at him. "Yes, Jake, I'll marry you."

Jake bent and kissed her mouth, lingering to savor the sweetness. "You want to get started on those kids tonight?"

Mina nodded. She felt as if she had been stuck on hold for too long, and it was time to move forward. Life happened whether you remained in step with it or not. Now she was going to get in step and keep moving.

In the bedroom, they removed their clothes and stood at the foot of the bed, wrapped in each other's arms, Mina's golden-brown skin tone contrasting nicely with Jake's darker brown.

She began kissing his chest and worked her way down to his six-pack, her hand delving even lower to grab hold of his semierect penis. The touch of her hand made him harden while she was holding him.

Mina ached with the need to have him inside of her. The prospect of creating a life with him sounded wonderful.

She pushed him onto the bed and got on top. He was so hard and she was so wet that he slipped right inside of her. Deeper and deeper he went, and the frequency and strength of the thrusts increased as time seemed to slow down. His hands were on her hips, massaging them, pressing her down and holding her in her sweet spot.

Jake couldn't take his eyes off Mina's face. She licked her lips, and that was an added turn-on for him. She threw her head back and thrust her breasts forward, which was nearly his undoing, but he held on. He was determined to hear her shout his name before he succumbed.

Mina's breath was coming in short bursts. She lifted her hair and let it fall down her back. Jake thought she looked like some primeval goddess, perhaps the goddess of love.

Her eyes had been closed as she savored every sensual aspect of the moment, but now she opened them and looked straight into his eyes. "Oh, Jake, I adore you!"

That did it for him. He came mightily, his seed shooting upward and into Mina. She collapsed on top of him. His arms went around her and held her tightly.

Jake didn't say it, but he was confident they'd just created a child together. And he couldn't wait to greet him or her.

The next morning Mina's family gathered in the cabin to have breakfast together before getting on the road to Raleigh. Jake was greeted with surprise, but no one inquired as to where he'd spent the night. The family simply arrived when Mina and Jake were in the middle of making pancakes, and everyone gathered in the kitchen to watch Jake flip the fluffy, delicious confections.

When Benjamin and Mabel arrived, Virginia offered them an apology for her behavior. She explained that she and Alfonse had been up practically all night talking, and she'd come to the conclusion that her reaction to their announcement yesterday had been due to the thought of her father forgetting her mother. It hadn't been because she believed Mabel to be a gold digger. Oftentimes, fear came out in the form of anger, and she sincerely regretted her actions.

"Baby girl, I could never forget your mother," Benjamin told her, opening his arms to her. Virginia walked into his embrace and cried fresh tears. "She'll always be a part of me," he assured her. He held her at arm's length. "Now, promise me that you'll be more patient with your family from now on. You're starting to get a reputation as a hard-ass."

Virginia laughed. "*Starting* to?"

Everyone laughed with her. After which she turned to Mabel and said, "Welcome to our family, Mabel."

Not one to stand on ceremony, Mabel grabbed the much smaller Virginia and hugged her to her ample bosom, nearly smothering her. When she was finally released, Virginia said breathlessly, "I guess that means I'm forgiven."

Mabel smiled. "No, you're grounded, young lady!"

Virginia burst out laughing.

Later, after everyone was seated around the table enjoying the pancakes, scrambled eggs and bacon that Mina and Jake had prepared, Jake, who was holding Mina's hand, said, while looking at the general, "Sir, I'd like to request your and Mrs. Gaines's permission to marry your daughter."

Pandemonium ensued as everyone began talking excitedly at once, getting up from their chairs to hug Mina and Jake and in general showing their support for them. Finally, they settled down enough to return to their chairs and speak calmly.

Alfonse sat with his arm draped about Virginia's shoulders, his eyes a bit misty. "I've only met you once before, son, so I can't say I know you well. But I know that if Mina loves you, you must be a good man. She doesn't give her heart to just anyone." He peered into his wife's smiling face. "I know Mina would object, but she's got a lot of her mother in her. She's fiercely loyal to family and will protect them with all her might. She's also one of the most determined women I've ever known. Once her mind is made up, nothing can stand in her way. Therefore, Ginny and I happily give our permission for you to marry Mina."

Jake got up and shook his hand, after which he and Mina kissed to seal the deal.

Later, as Mina walked Desiree and Meghan to the Hummer in preparation for their trip back to Raleigh, Mina told Meghan what Jake had told her about Leo.

Meghan's face brightened. "He really likes me, too?"

"He does," Mina confirmed. "Now, armed with that knowledge, it's up to you to do something about it."

"Oh, I most certainly will," Meghan said with conviction.

Mina liked the sound of that. She hugged both sisters goodbye and watched as her father started the Hummer. She, Jake, her grandfather and Miss Mabel stood waving as the Hummer and the Range Rover motored away from the lodge.

Mina and Jake decided on a simple wedding at the lodge. They both loved it, and since it was to be their home for the foreseeable future, they wanted to begin their life together there. Benjamin, who had returned from a honeymoon in Hawaii with Mabel two weeks earlier with his heart set on retirement, had turned the lodge fully over to Mina. He and Mabel, he said, were going to travel.

The December morning Mina and Jake were to be wed loomed clear and cold. But, luckily, the weather service wasn't predicting snow. Mina learned this when she got up and turned on the TV for the morning news. Her parents and her sisters were staying with her, so she tried to be as quiet as possible as she sat on the couch and watched the news in the living room.

She didn't even notice her mother entering the room until Virginia had sat down beside her. Virginia wore a robe over her nightgown. Mina wore pajamas.

"It's your big day. Nervous?" Virginia asked, a smile tugging at the corners of her mouth.

Mina smiled at her mother. "No," she said with no hesitation. "Not at all."

Virginia reached over and affectionately grasped her daughter's hand. "I'm glad. That means you have no doubts." She took a deep breath. "He's a good guy, your Jake. And the fact that you've both lost people you love will make you appreciate each other that much more. I'm happy for you, my love."

Mina brought her mother's hand to her cheek. "Thank you, Momma."

Virginia's eyes roamed over Mina's hair. "Are you going to let me fix your hair today? It's getting to be a tradition, you know."

"I wouldn't want to break with tradition," Mina replied good-naturedly.

At two o'clock, only minutes before the ceremony was to start, the weather was splendid with a cloudless blue sky and the temperature in the fifties. A breeze wafting off the pines reminded the guests that they were in the middle of a forest.

Chairs had been placed on either side of an aisle in the main lobby of the lodge. A hundred guests were already seated in them, conversing among themselves, their voices like a low hum.

Upstairs Mina had been helped into her wedding dress by her mother, Meghan, Desiree and Lauren, who'd given birth to a beautiful baby boy twenty days previously.

Now Mina was sitting in front of a vanity while her mother piled her braids atop her head in an upswept style. She took a moment to look around the room at the happy faces of her loved ones. The only sister missing was Petra, who hadn't been able to come due to work. She was in the middle of the jungle in central Africa. They'd spoken via Skype, and Petra wished her well and promised to be home in a few months to meet her new brother-in-law.

"Let me see that sweet face one more time before I go downstairs," Mina said to Lauren, who was cuddling Colton Junior in her arms. Lauren came and lowered the blanket so CJ's Aunt Mina could peer into his scrunched-up little face. He was sleeping, as usual. Mina sighed longingly over him. He looked like a miniature Colton with that milk-chocolate-colored skin and dark brown hair, but when he opened his eyes they were his mother's dark brown instead of his father's gray.

Mina's hand went instinctively to her flat belly.

She'd missed her period. Maybe Colton Junior would have a cousin to play with soon.

She rose and said to the women gathered around her, "You all look so beautiful, you're going to put the bride to shame."

"Don't be ridiculous," their mother exclaimed. "Nobody outshines the bride on her wedding day!"

Her sisters were visions in off-white, wearing various styles of knee-length dresses that fit their particular bodies to perfection. Her mother wore a tailored pantsuit in the same shade. Mina wore white. Hers was a strapless gown whose hem fell a couple of inches above her knees.

Desiree stepped forward and handed her a small bouquet of fragrant miniature pink roses, Mina's favorite flowers.

"Something new," Desiree intoned as she handed them over.

"These are your grandmother's pearl earrings," Virginia said as she reached up to place them in Mina's ears. "They're something old and something borrowed."

"And here's something blue," Meghan said, twirling a fancy blue garter around her finger. "I'm sure Jake will enjoy taking this off you at the right moment."

She bent, and Mina put her right foot through the circle of the stretchy garter and held up the hem of her dress to work it all the way up her thigh. She put down her dress's hem. "Okay, I think I'm ready now."

Desiree held the door open for her. "Go and get him, sis!"

Her sisters giggled, but soon got their laughter under control when their mother gave them a fierce look. "This is supposed to be a dignified ceremony, ladies. Check yourselves."

Mina's father was waiting on the landing to escort her downstairs. Her mother quickly went and sat down. Then the processional began and her sisters, her bridesmaids, descended the stairs on the arms of three groomsmen, one of whom was Jake's best man, Leo. Mina had made sure he was partnered with Meghan.

Mina's eyes were drawn to Jake as she descended the stairs on her father's arm. He was so handsome in his black tux. He was beaming at her. She beamed back, feeling giddy with happiness.

As Mina came toward them, Leo whispered in Jake's ear, "You lucky dog. She's gorgeous!"

Jake's smile just broadened. He knew how lucky he was to have found Mina. Or perhaps it was the other way around. She had found him. Either way, they were together now, and that's what counted.

At last, Alfonse placed Mina's hand in Jake's and murmured, "Be happy, you two," after which he went and sat down beside Virginia.

The minister, a Cherokee man in his sixties with long gray hair tied back in a ponytail, began the ceremony. "Dearly beloved, we are gathered here today to unite in holy matrimony…"

Mina was lost in Jake's eyes. She heard the minister's words, and responded accordingly, but her attention was focused on Jake and the loving manner in which he was watching her. She heard the minister say, "You may kiss your bride," and then Jake was kissing her to thunderous applause. He swept her off her feet and carried her down the aisle while the guests shouted words of congratulations at them.

Later, as Mina and Jake waltzed under the afternoon sun on the raised platform that had been erected for the occasion, she looked out over the crowd and spotted everyone she loved, save Petra, having a good time. Jake's parents and grandparents had traveled from Florida. They were down-to-earth people with genuine warmth and compassion, and she'd immediately fallen in love with them. She saw them now talking with her parents and grandparents.

"Your folks look like they're enjoying themselves," she said to Jake.

He was gazing down at her, his love for her apparent in his expression. "They are," he said softly. "This turned out to be some party, huh?"

Mina smiled. "The best of my life."

Jake bent and kissed her. When they came up for air and continued their waltz, Jake held her close and said, "Maybe this time next year we'll have a third dance partner."

Mina imagined them waltzing around the dance floor with an infant held between them.

"One can only hope," she said with a contented sigh.

* * * * *

A sizzling new miniseries set in the wide-open spaces of Montana!

THE BROWARDS OF MONTANA
Passionate love in the West

JACQUELIN THOMAS	DARA GIRARD	HARMONY EVANS

WRANGLING WES	ENGAGING BROOKE	LOVING LANEY
Available April 2014	*Available May 2014*	*Available June 2014*

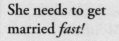

REQUEST YOUR FREE BOOKS!

2 FREE NOVELS
PLUS 2 FREE GIFTS!

KIMANI™
ROMANCE

Love's ultimate destination!